Fire

www.penguin.co.uk

Also by John Boyne

Fire

JOHN BOYNE

doubleday

TRANSWORLD PUBLISHERS
Penguin Random House, One Embassy Gardens,
8 Viaduct Gardens, London sw11 7bw
www.penguin.co.uk

Transworld is part of the Penguin Random House group of companies
whose addresses can be found at global.penguinrandomhouse.com

First published in Great Britain in 2024 by Doubleday
an imprint of Transworld Publishers

Lyrics on p.161 from 'It Started With A Kiss' by Hot Chocolate,
written by Errol Brown

Every effort has been made to obtain the necessary permissions with
reference to copyright material, both illustrative and quoted. We apologize
for any omissions in this respect and will be pleased to make the
appropriate acknowledgements in any future edition.

A CIP catalogue record for this book
is available from the British Library.

ISBN 9780857529879

Typeset in 11/14.5pt Dante MT Std by Jouve (UK), Milton Keynes
Printed and bound in Great Britain by Clays Ltd, Elcograf S.p.A.

The authorized representative in the EEA is Penguin Random House Ireland,
Morrison Chambers, 32 Nassau Street, Dublin D02 YH68.

Penguin Random House is committed to a sustainable future
for our business, our readers and our planet. This book is made
from Forest Stewardship Council® certified paper.

I

WHEN I WAS TWELVE years old, I was buried alive within the grounds of a construction site.

Ever since, I've been terrified of enclosed spaces and one of the consequences of this is that I always try to avoid elevators. This morning, however, workmen are repairing the staircase between the ground and first floors of the hospital, leaving me with no choice but to make my way up to the burns unit in the lift. And, to make matters worse, I'm not alone.

The boy standing in the corner can't be more than fourteen and he appears anxious, tapping his right foot on the floor in an insistent rhythm. I try to intuit from his demeanour whether he's visiting a loved one or is here for a consultation himself and decide on the former. Next to him stands an overweight man with a heavily stubbled double chin who I assume is his father. When he catches my eye, he holds it for a moment before allowing his gaze to fall to my breasts. As we ascend through the spinal column of the building, he continues to stare, before looking up and studying my face, as if he's deciding whether or not, given the opportunity, he would have sex with me. When he looks away and yawns, I can only assume that I haven't met his exacting standards.

They exit on the fourth floor – Renal – while I continue up to the sixth, exhaling in relief when the doors finally open, a slight prickle of perspiration tickling my back. Ahead of me stands Louise Shaw, the most senior nurse practitioner and the closest thing I have to a friend here, along with Aaron Umber, a medical student who's taken the unusual step of opting for a three-month elective on my team. He's my responsibility, but for some reason his presence has irritated me since his arrival. He's never anything but polite and is both diligent in his work and focused on our patients, so I have no reason to feel such antipathy towards him, but nevertheless, I find myself snapping whenever the poor lad opens his mouth.

'Good morning,' says Louise, somehow managing to control the dozen or so files that she's carrying, along with the Styrofoam cup of coffee and KitKat with which she greets me every morning. She's due to retire soon and I'm worried that whoever replaces her will not be as attentive to my needs. 'Late night?'

'No,' I say. 'Why do you ask?'

'You look tired.'

'Thank you. It's always nice to start the day being told that I look wretched.'

'I didn't say that you looked wretched,' she tells me, her Irish accent seeping through. 'I said you looked tired. There's a difference.'

'Well, as it happens, I was in bed by ten,' I tell her, which is the truth, although I wasn't alone, so perhaps that accounts for any weariness I'm exhibiting. I turn to Aaron, who's watching me in that unsettling way of his, as if he suspects I'm not human at all but a visitor from another planet, and not a particularly friendly one at that. It's crossed my mind that he might have a crush on me. I'm only thirty-six, after all, and from what the media are always telling me, young men his age are consumed these days with lust for older women. Leaving aside the fact that I'm his superior, however, he hasn't a chance as he's not even remotely my type. It's not that he's unattractive – in fact, he's quite good-looking, if you like that sort of thing, with dark blond hair cut high on his head and short at the sides and sharp, grey eyes – but he's thirteen years my junior and I haven't slept with a twenty-three-year-old since I *was* twenty-three and have no intention of ever doing so again.

'What do you think, Aaron?' I ask him. 'Am I some washed-out old hag?'

'You look fine, Dr Petrus,' he tells me, his cheeks colouring a little at the directness of my question.

'Just fine?'

'No, you look great. I mean . . .' He trails off, clearly uncomfortable with this line of questioning. One good thing about the contemporary world, where everyone lives in perpetual hope that they'll be on the receiving end of a remark deemed sufficiently offensive that it can be reported to HR, is that conversations between colleagues, particularly between those of opposite sexes, tend to remain professional. Which suits me fine.

'You ignore her,' Louise instructs Aaron with a maternal smile before turning back to me. 'You'll want these,'
she adds, extending the pile of folders in her arms. 'Just
the usual. Test results, evaluations, overnights, and so on.'

'Put them on my desk, will you, Aaron?' I ask, retriev-
ing the coffee and KitKat and watching as he scurries
along the corridor. His trainers have seen better days and,
as he's quite tall, his ill-fitting scrubs expose his ankles.
Maybe it's the fashion these days.

'How much longer do I have to deal with him?' I ask
when he's out of earshot.

'Not much longer than you have to deal with me,' she
says. 'But, of course, after he's gone, another him will show
up. Along with another me. We're all replaceable.'

'Another you would be fine. Another him though . . .'

'Be nice,' she says, admonishing me in the way that
only she would have the courage to do. 'You intimidate
him, that's all. You look like a supermodel, speak like
a fishwife, and, on top of that, you're his boss. That's a
combination that frightens boys his age.'

'He's not a boy,' I tell her. 'He's a man. There's a
difference.'

We exchange a few particulars about a skin graft I'll be
performing just after lunch on a young woman who col-
lapsed with an arrhythmia, ending up with third-degree
burns from the two-bar electric heater that warmed her
flat because she couldn't afford anything more. Then I
make my way towards my office, hoping that Aaron
won't be waiting inside for me. My prayers are answered
because he's vanished off to wherever he takes himself

when I'm not barking orders at him. The precision with which he's laid out the folders on my desk annoys me, and then the fact that it annoys me annoys me too. It's ridiculous that I should be so aggravated by his efficiency.

I follow through on some emails, sending quick, straight-forward replies to anything that seems urgent. A conference taking place in Paris in a few months' time that has invited me to present a paper on the ethics of temporary grafts from deceased donors. A medical journal asking whether I might proofread an article on the prevalence of oedemas in over sixty-fives who've suffered insult to the top two layers of the dermis. Various administrative hospital matters, including details of a meeting where I'm invited to discuss what further cuts I can make in my department to help ensure that the NHS runs on a budget of about £2.99 a day. An hour passes, and as I do my rounds at eleven thirty, which is fast approaching, I reach into my bag, grab my cigarettes and lighter, and head back towards the dreaded elevator, passing Aaron on the way and telling him to be ready to join me on my return.

It's a warm morning and I'd intended standing in my usual spot just under the shade of the awning, but, seated on a bench about twenty feet away, near the statue of the hospital's founder – who was involved in the nineteenth-century slave trade, although no one's cottoned on to that yet, so he remains *in situ* for now – I notice the boy from earlier. He's alone, his elbows on his knees, his head in his hands, staring at the ground. I know that I should turn away, smoke my cigarette in peace, and focus on this afternoon's operation, but when I see a boy his age in such obvious pain and showing clear signs of vulnerability, I simply can't help myself.

'Do you mind?' I ask as I approach him, and he startles for a moment, before looking up and shaking his head. His straight dark hair tumbles down to his eyebrows, a little like The Beatles in their mop-top days. His skin is mercifully free of acne, but his nails are a horror to behold. He must gnaw on them like a teething puppy with a chew-toy. In fact, he lifts his left hand to his mouth as I sit, attacking his index finger with gusto, and I gently slap it away. 'Don't do that,' I tell him with a smile, so he knows I'm not just being a scold. 'You never know what kind of bacteria you're carrying on there.'

'That's what my mum says,' he tells me. 'She also says that smoking causes cancer.'

I turn to look at him and raise an eyebrow.

'Cute,' I say, taking my first drag, then blowing the smoke towards him, and he waves a hand in the air to drive it away. I hold the flame of the lighter steady for a few moments, enjoying its purple-blue splendour, before snapping the cap shut. Reaching for the pack, I offer it in his direction.

'I'm fourteen,' he tells me, a note of reproach in his voice. When did teenagers become so puritanical? At his age, I would have taken one and put a second behind my ear for later.

'I won't tell if you don't.'

'No, thanks,' he says.

We remain silent for a few moments and when it becomes obvious that he's too shy to talk, I take the lead.

Which is fine. I'm no paediatrician, but I do know how to talk to boys his age. I've made quite a study of it.

'I saw you in the lift earlier, didn't I?' I ask him. 'You looked a little upset. Was that your dad with you?'

'Yes.'

'Are you sick? I'm not prying. I'm a doctor. I work here.'

'No, I'm fine,' he tells me. 'It's my friend. He's not doing so well.'

'Who's your friend?'

'Harry Cullimore. Do you know him?'

I shake my head and take another drag on my cigarette. The name means nothing to me, but then the hospital has almost 180 beds and I rarely venture far from either the burns unit or A&E. He tells me that Harry had a kidney transplant three months earlier, but it hasn't taken and he's back on dialysis now, waiting for some unlucky person to crash their motorbike or fall under a bus. He's been kept in for the last five days due to complications related to a bladder infection and there's no sign of him being released any time soon. When he says the word 'bladder', he blushes and looks away, which is adorable.

'It's good of you to visit him,' I say.

'He's my best mate,' he replies with a shrug. 'We grew up together.'

The boy is close to tears and his helplessness touches me.

'And you?' I ask. 'What's your name?'

'George,' he says.

'George what?'

'George Eliot.'

I laugh, unsure whether he's joking.

'What?' he asks.

'George Eliot?' I ask. 'Seriously?'

'Oh yeah,' he tells me, obviously accustomed to being asked this question. 'The writer. I know. But she was a woman, wasn't she? And I'm, you know, not.'

'That's really your name?'

He nods, and I have no reason to doubt him. It would be a strange thing to invent.

'Well, I'm Freya,' I say, offering him my hand to shake. He takes it, although he's obviously uncomfortable with such an adult convention. His palm is slick with perspiration and I try to be subtle when I wipe it on my skirt. 'Where's your dad anyway? Is he coming back to collect you?'

'No, he had to go back to work. He just dropped me off and came up to say hi to Harry. I'll get the bus home in a bit. You don't work in the kidney department, do you?'

'No,' I say. 'Burns.'

'Like, people caught in fires?'

'Among other things, yes.'

He grimaces, as people often do when I tell them my speciality. Illnesses are one thing, but disfigurements, particularly those caused by fire, make people uncomfortable. They feel sympathy for the victims, of course, but they'd prefer not to witness the deformities.

'Are there things the doctors aren't telling him?' he asks. 'Harry, I mean. Could you find out and let me know?'

'I'm sorry, no,' I say. 'I can't do that.'

'Why not? He's my best mate,' he repeats.

'I understand. But there are rules regarding patient confidentiality. You'll have to speak to your friend himself.

Or his parents. I'm sure he'll share with you whatever his doctors have told him.'

He nods. He's seen enough television shows to know the ethics that govern the medical profession. I'm aware of his eyes drifting towards my legs. He isn't any more subtle in his ogling than his father was, just less experienced in it. His tongue protrudes from his mouth and I know that, right now, he's not thinking about Harry. He's thinking about sex. But then, to my surprise, he starts crying.

'Hey,' I say, stubbing my cigarette out beneath my trainer and moving closer to him. 'Are you OK?'

'Yeah,' he says, wiping the tears from his cheeks. 'Sorry. It's just—'

'What?'

'I don't want him to die.'

I am rarely troubled by sentiment. I prefer to remain dispassionate in my dealings with patients and their families, speaking to them in ways that neither patronize nor offer false hope. I tell the truth, refusing to sugarcoat adverse diagnoses. When I have to deal with the emotions of children who have suffered in conflagrations, their skin blistered, their features distorted, their nerve endings either severed or screaming out in unendurable pain, I do so in the company of their parents and a nurse – usually Louise – along with one of the hospital's paediatric therapists, where I remain composed and professional throughout. So I'm surprised when George's tears inspire an unfamiliar and, if I'm honest, rather unwelcome empathy in me.

'I'm sure your friend's doctors are doing everything they can for him,' I say.

'Do people die from kidney failure a lot?' he asks.

'It happens,' I admit. 'It's a serious disease. But older people, mostly. Your friend's body will be young and healthy, so he has that in his favour. It will put up a fight.'

'He doesn't look healthy. His face is grey and he's all weak. Like, he can't even get out of bed on his own right now.'

There's not much I can say to reassure him. The truth is, if Harry has already rejected one kidney, then he will most likely reject another. Multiple transplants cause extraordinary trauma and bodies as young as his aren't designed to be abused. Eventually, without renal attainment, his functioning organs will be unable to compensate and they'll start to shut down. Of course, I don't say any of this to George. He wants comfort, not a professional opinion.

'It's good that you care about your friend so much,' I tell him. 'It's sweet.'

He studiously avoids looking at me. Teenage boys never want to look fragile in front of girls or women. When they talk about us with their friends, they can be ruthless and demeaning, speaking of us as little more than bodies to be used or experimented upon for their pleasure, but when they're alone with someone of the opposite sex, their intrinsic terror and total spinelessness assert themselves. They are monsters, every one of them, utterly devoid of decency.

'I sometimes have to treat people your and Harry's age,' I tell him, cautiously placing a hand on his while not wanting to frighten him away. His skin is incredibly soft. 'And every one of them feels better when they know they have people who care about them. You could be out with your other friends right now, larking around, having fun. But instead, you're here. He's lucky to have you.'

There's something I want to ask him, but I made a promise to myself when I woke this morning that I would never ask this question of anyone again. To break that vow within a few hours would show a total lack of will-power on my part. And so I simply glance at my watch and stand up. I need to go. Rounds.

'You take care of yourself, George Eliot,' I say. Turning my back on him, I feel his eyes follow me as I walk away. He's upset, concerned for his friend's well-being, but he's still a fourteen-year-old boy and his hormones are affecting his every waking moment. Ahead of me are the sliding doors that will lead me back inside and I tell myself to keep walking, to march through them, return to the elevator, and let him go about his day.

But that's when I think of Arthur and Pascoe, of the caves dotted around the coastline of Cornwall, of the night I almost died, and I'm defenceless. I stop, look down at the ground for a moment, then close my eyes, allowing myself a resigned sigh. When I open them again and turn around, George looks away, embarrassed at being caught staring, and I walk back towards him.

He has nothing to fear. If anything, it's me who should be afraid.

After all, a doctor in the burns unit should know better than to play with fire.

2

I'VE NEVER HEARD THE name Vidar before and so, as we make our way downstairs, I ask Aaron to google it. After some quick fumbling with his phone, he tells me that Vidar was the Norse god of vengeance, which feels somehow appropriate, considering the conversation I plan on having with the parents of a four-year-old child I've just finished treating.

'How are you with kids?' I ask him.

'Good in the sense that I like them,' he tells me. 'Bad in the sense that I can't bear to see them hurt.'

'They wouldn't be here if they weren't hurt,' I reply. 'It's not like they come here just for the fun of it. We're not Euro Disney.'

He throws me a look that suggests he's formulated an equally sarcastic reply in his head but doesn't quite have the confidence to deliver it yet.

As we approach the second floor, I relate to him the boy's past presentations. He's been treated in A&E twice over the last twelve months, once for a broken wrist (left), when he fell off his tricycle, and once for a perforated eardrum (right), after he stuck a pencil so far into his ear canal that it breached the tympanic membrane.

Now, only twelve weeks later, he's back with a deep dermal burn to his right hand after supposedly pressing it against one of the hobs on the family's electric stove. There's no record of any further investigation being done into the child's well-being after the second episode, and for a third to take place in such a short time frame raises red flags.

'That doesn't seem like something a child would do,' says Aaron. 'Children don't seek out pain. They run from it.'

'Most,' I say.

'All,' he insists.

'Well, yes,' I concede. Anyone can let their hand fall upon a hotplate, but the body's natural aversion to trauma makes it physically impossible for it to remain there, any more than we can strangle ourselves or force ourselves to remain under the water level in a bath. 'To suffer a burn this deep, someone must have held him down.'

'Jesus,' he says, visibly disgusted, and his revulsion is not just performative; I can tell that he means it. 'Don't you wonder what kind of person would hurt a child?'

'You obviously haven't done your paeds rotation yet,' I tell him. 'When you do, you'll see exactly the sort of people who do things like that. Most of the time, they're called parents.'

'Not always though.'

'No.'

The boy's father, Börje, who's Swedish, looks anxious when he sees me marching down the corridor, as well he might, because if he thinks I'm going to fall for whatever ridiculous version of events he's invented to explain what's taken place here, then he's delusional. I don't even waste my time saying hello, simply raise a finger to point him towards a nearby room, where his wife, Sharon, is already seated, cradling the boy on her lap. The child is subdued, nursing a dummy in his mouth, his eyes half closed, barely alert. Soft, wounded whimpers escape him from time to time, like an animal caught in a trap who's slowly losing the will to fight on.

Exhausted both from the medications he's been given and the ordeal he's going through, his central nervous system is working overtime to force him to sleep. When I examined the burn earlier, a large blister had already developed on the palm of his hand and the damage to the subcutaneous blood vessels had turned the skin alabaster white. Thankfully, the attending nurse had given him a shot to relieve what must have been unbearable pain, but even he, who must see harrowing injuries on a daily basis, looked upset by the child's distress. I gave instructions for the wound to be cleaned, dressed, and treated with a course of silver sulfadiazine, before asking to meet the parents privately to clarify the chain of events that led their son here.

'So, what happened?' I ask without any preamble, pausing for only a moment before adding, 'This time.'

A silver box sits on the table in the centre of the room with tissues peeping from the top, while a portrait of the king and queen, wearing comforting expressions, hangs on the wall. This is the room where people are brought to be told that a loved one has died. It's where A&E doctors explain to shocked relatives why they were unable to save a life, directing them towards ancillary staff who can instruct them on what to do next before fleeing in search of patients still breathing. I take a seat, but Aaron, I notice, remains standing by the wall, his arms crossed before him in a surprisingly aggressive gesture. His attention is directed towards the child, who he's studying with real compassion on his face. I can't decide whether this degree of empathy will ultimately make him a good doctor or a terrible one.

'He was playing,' says Börje. 'Seeing how long he could keep his hand on the cooker.'

The man's English is almost perfect, tinged with just a slight Scandinavian accent.

'I don't accept that,' I say, shaking my head. 'It's not something that anyone could possibly do, let alone a child. So I ask again: what happened? The truth, this time.'

Börje glances down at the floor. A neck tattoo is visible, descending beneath his polo shirt towards his back. Ropes of some sort. I don't know what they signify. He's a powerfully built man, shaven-headed, thick-necked, muscular, shoulders straining to be released from beneath the cotton fabric. His son's file tells me that he's a construction worker, which might go some way to explain my immediate antipathy to him, as it recalls memories of Arthur and Pascoe, and the building site in Cornwall where they buried me alive. But he does not frighten me. Men do not frighten me. If anything, it's them who should feel nervous.

'He can be naughty,' explains Börje, and his choice of word is another indication that he's not completely familiar with the nuances of English, for I can't remember the last time I heard a child described in such an old-fashioned way. Vidar snuffles a little in his mother's arms, halfway between consciousness and sleep. He doesn't know what's going on, only that he's suffered before, he's suffering now, and most likely he'll suffer again. This is his life. It has probably been this way since the day he was born.

'Your son has third-degree burns,' I say. 'There's a chance that he'll never have full feeling in his hand again.'

The man's face falls. He looks frightened, traumatized, grief-stricken, all at once. Whatever fit of rage led him to do this to the boy, it has passed now, and he's witnessing the result of his actions. This will not end well for him, I tell myself, taking some pleasure in drawing out his pain, wanting to inflict as much distress on him as he has on this defenceless child. I will let it slowly dawn on him that I know what he has done and that I intend to make him pay for it. When I'm ready, I will call the police and see to it that he's arrested. I will testify against him in court, as I've done many times before. I will do all I can to ensure that he never hurts his son again.

'We should go home,' says Börje, his voice trembling, and it disgusts me to witness the hypocrisy of the tears pooling in his eyes.

'No, not yet,' I say, making it clear that he's not in charge; I am. 'I need to know exactly what happened here. This is your last chance to tell me the truth.'

'I already have,' he insists. 'The cooker, the electric heat—'

'A child cannot inflict that level of trauma on himself,' I insist, raising my voice. 'It's ridiculous of you even to suggest it.'

I mean trauma in the medical sense, of course, not the emotional. Although I can only guess at how much distress this small boy has endured in his short life. He must believe that the world is a place he entered only to be hurt. He must long for release. In his mother's arms, he cries out and tries to sit up, but, to my astonishment, when she attempts to comfort him, he reaches out to his thug of a father before a burst of pain in his hand makes him explode in near-hysterical tears. I've seen this before. He wants Börje because if he can convince the man that he will be good from now on, then the man might never hurt him again.

'How long do we need to stay here?' asks the mother, Sharon, and I turn to study her for the first time. She's English, a plain sort of woman, overweight but dressing to disguise it, with dry skin and dark bags beneath her eyes. Although she's younger than me, she could pass for ten years older. I wonder how she can allow this man, this husband, this person who she once went on dates with, and laughed with, and fell in love with, and slept with, and holidayed with, and got pregnant with, and had a child with – how she can let him hurt her little boy in the way that he has.

'As long as it takes,' I say, softening my tone now, for I don't want her to feel any worse than she already must. 'This is the third time that Vidar has presented in a year, Mrs Forsberg. That gives us cause for concern.'

'He is a mischievous boy,' says Börje.

'A mischievous boy,' I repeat, shaking my head, almost laughing. I wonder where he picks up these phrases.

'But a good boy,' he adds, looking directly at me. There's something in his eyes. Something pained. Something asking me to – what? Forgive him? Accept that he doesn't mean to do the things he does to his own child, but that he has no choice?

Fuck you, I think.

I will destroy your life.

I will bury you alive.

'He's tired,' says Sharon, lifting the child slightly off her lap. 'He needs to be in his own bed.'

'No,' I say. 'Not yet.'

'Then when?'

I turn back to Börje.

'When you tell me the truth.'

'I've told you,' he insists. 'I've—'

'No,' I say. 'You can forget that. Your explanation makes no sense. So you can tell me everything now, or I can go outside and call the police and let them get to the bottom of it. It's your choice.'

I turn back to Sharon, willing her to set aside whatever fear she might feel towards her husband. What violence has he inflicted upon her? I wonder. If she were to remove her clothes, what scars or bruises would I discover on her body? Using only my eyes, I try to tell her that I can protect her too, if only she trusts me.

From her bag comes the sound of a phone ringing. To my surprise, she retrieves it, answers it, and talks to the

caller as if nothing that is taking place in this room matters in the slightest. And as she does so, the child remains
in her arms, weeping softly, unaware of the pain that will
come in the middle of the night, or the following morning, when the painkillers have worn off.

'Börje,' says Sharon, passing the boy roughly towards
her husband. The child is like a rag doll, his limbs flop-
ping uselessly. 'It's Sara. Take him, will you?'

'Whoever Sara is, she can wait,' says Aaron, speaking
for the first time since we gathered here. His tone mixes
authority with controlled rage. I turn to look at him, surprised by his intervention. 'This is more important.'

'Sara is my boss,' replies Sharon irritably, waving him
away as if he's utterly insignificant. 'I can't just ignore her.'

Honestly, I'm surprised that she works at all. She looks
like one of those women who sits at home all day, watching daytime television programmes that tell her how to
make tasty, healthy meals for her family, using ingredi-
ents she couldn't possibly afford, let alone source, before
frying fish fingers for her son and throwing a few cheese
strings on the plate. In this moment, I feel as much antag-
onism towards her as I do towards her husband. They
deserve each other, but Vidar doesn't deserve either
of them.

'When I come back,' says Sharon, standing up and
walking towards the door, 'we really have to go.' She's
addressing me now like I'm the help. 'So, can you just get
my son everything he needs, please? His medications or
creams or whatever? We can take care of him from here.
We're his parents, after all.'

She doesn't wait for a reply, just walks out, turning her attention back to her phone and letting the door swing closed behind her.

The room falls into silence for the best part of a minute, until:

'Help us,' whispers Börje.

'What?' I ask, uncertain whether I have heard him right.

'Help us,' he repeats, still beneath his breath, as if he's too frightened even to let me hear what he's saying. 'Please. You must help us.'

At first, I don't understand what he means, but then he glances towards the window that faces out on to the corridor, where his wife is gesticulating wildly on her phone, before standing up, carrying Vidar over to Aaron and placing the child in my intern's arms. The boy turns his head, muttering something unintelligible, before nestling into Aaron's chest. Sharon has disappeared now, but still, Börje moves away from the window and towards the wall, where he cannot be seen from outside, before turning his back on me. Slowly, he pulls his polo shirt up, dragging the hem towards the base of his neck tattoo, exposing his back, which is covered with purple bruises and scratches. Someone has hurt him too. Someone has beaten this powerfully built man and he has not been able or willing to ward off the blows. I study his injuries. They are terrible. They need medical attention. And they are, of course, hidden in a place where others cannot see them. Once he's certain that I understand, he lets his shirt fall again and turns back to me.

'Help us,' he repeats. 'Please.'

And it's only now that I glance outside and see Sharon marching back towards us, her face contorted with anger, looking as if she will not accept another moment of defiance from either her husband, her child, Aaron, or me.

That's when I understand what is actually going on here.

That it's not always the man who is the offender.

That women can be abusers too.

I look at Börje, but before I can say anything, Aaron pipes up.

'Of course,' he says, for some reason excluding me in what he says next. 'Of course I'll help you.'

3

FRIDAY EVENING. AN EMPTY weekend stretches out before me, which might explain why, after making my final check of post-operative patients in the late afternoon, my compulsion takes hold. I consider going to the cinema, but the idea of sitting in a darkened auditorium for two hours doesn't appeal. I could take a book to my local wine bar, but some man will inevitably approach to tell me that a gorgeous woman like me shouldn't be drinking alone, and when I make it clear that I'm not interested, he'll insist on buying me a glass of wine anyway. When I say I don't want one, he'll reply that I've probably never tried a Sequoia Grove Cambium, and he knows they have some bottles of the 2006 here and he's not taking no for an answer. When I say he'll have to, he'll shake his head and tell me to trust him, that I'll thank him when I try it. And when I tell him to please go away, to please just leave me the fuck alone, he'll stare at me with an expression suggesting that he'd like to pin me to the wall by the throat and inform me that it's my loss, he was only trying to be friendly, and that I'd be a lot prettier if I smiled. The whole thing will leave me in such a murderous rage that it's simply masochistic to put myself through the ordeal.

In a vain attempt to ward off my urges, and knowing that this usually has a soporific effect on me, I order a meal from a local Indian restaurant, but only pick at it, leaving most of the food in the fridge to be reheated for tomorrow's lunch.

Finally, accepting my weakness, I take a long, hot shower, tie my hair back into a ponytail, and apply a little make-up before dressing in a pair of blue jeans and a simple white blouse. Hanging a sapphire pendant around my neck, I examine myself in the mirror and smile. I was a reasonably attractive teenager, but I became more striking in my twenties, and now, in my mid-thirties, I've some-how become beautiful. Almost every heterosexual doctor in the hospital has hit on me at one time or another, but I've knocked them all back. I've heard whispers that people think I might be a closeted lesbian, and it irritates me to think they believe I'd be so shallow as to conceal something of such little consequence. For a while, I invented a boyfriend as my excuse to decline invitations for drinks, visits to art galleries, or trips to upcoming con-certs. My fantasy lover's name was Jesse, he was two years younger than me, a windsurfing fanatic whose man-bun was something I ruthlessly mocked but secretly adored. We met on a train when we were travelling sep-arately towards Vienna and ended up spending the entire night wandering the city, telling each other the story of our lives. I lifted the entire plot of our romance from an old movie, but if anyone noticed they didn't mention it. Jesse and I were together for a few years, until he left me for a younger woman. You know things are bad when even your imaginary boyfriend cheats on you.

It's not that I haven't tried dating. When I was in my final year of medical school, I went out with a first-year student who was planning a career in thoracic surgery. At first, I enjoyed his company, but, as I got to know him better, I realized that all he cared about was the money he would eventually make, the house he would eventually buy, the luxury holidays he would eventually go on. He was only twenty but could spend an entire evening discussing his pension plan. When he announced that he'd purchased a space in a cemetery's memorial wall where his ashes would be placed after his death, and suggested we visit it together on a Sunday afternoon, I broke up with him.

Later, when I was qualified, I tried something completely out of character, having an affair with a married anaesthesiologist some twenty years my senior, but try as I might, I couldn't enjoy the sex. Louise tells me that if I'm not careful, I'll end up on the shelf, like the responsible eldest sister in a Jane Austen novel, but the truth is, I'd rather tie a noose around my neck than place a ring on my finger.

I spray a little perfume on my neck and wrists and, before leaving the flat, make sure to leave my purse on the dressing table in the bedroom. I turn on the lamp in the living room as it will offer a welcoming glow when I, or we, return. Also, I check there's a can of Coke in the fridge. I hate Coke and never drink the stuff, but on nights like these it's important that there's one waiting.

The building I live in lies on the outskirts of the city, fourteen storeys high, and my apartment is on the twelfth. I have far more room than I need, but a feeling of space is important to me. I can't be closed in. If the regulations permitted it, I would knock down every wall and turn it into a 2,500-square-foot studio apartment, but under the terms of my lease, internal reconstruction is prohibited. When I first viewed it, I was hesitant to commit as the estate agent informed me that it had once been owned by a well-known footballer. By a strange coincidence, I had sat on the jury for the young man's rape trial some years earlier and worried that this might prove a bad omen. In the end, however, I decided that it was too good to give up and, after all, the offence hadn't taken place here but in the building opposite.

In the underground garage, I'm walking towards my car when I see Hugh Winley coming towards me. Hugh moved into the apartment above my own earlier this year and, unlike the other residents, who tend to keep themselves to themselves, has an irritating habit of trying to engage me in conversation. I've done my best to keep him at bay while not being rude, but he's persistent. A children's television presenter, he seems to think that makes him something special, or that I should think he's something special, which I don't.

'Freya,' he says, picking up his pace to catch up with me. 'Where have you been? I haven't seen you in ages.'

'I've been working,' I say.

'Of course. Busy busy,' he replies, nodding furiously and pulling at the neck of his low-cut T-shirt to ensure that I can see the definition of his pectoral muscles. 'I've hardly had a minute to myself lately either. I was at a reception for the Prince's Trust last night and—'

'Can't stop,' I tell him, not wanting to suffer his attempts to impress me by name-dropping whatever nineties pop star or self-aggrandizing former *Hollyoaks* actor he ran into there. 'Another time, yes?'

He moves around rather deftly, inserting himself between me and the car door so I can't open it without physically pushing him out of the way. Like many men, he's not trying to appear threatening but is making it clear that he has no intention of letting me leave until he's completed whatever pathetic mission he's on.

'Actually, I'm glad I caught up with you,' he continues. 'There was something I wanted to ask you.'

I offer a deep sigh. It's easier just to let him spit it out.

'Have you ever heard of Aladdin Stardust?'

I have no idea what he's talking about. It sounds like some sort of Christmas pantomime, but, as it's only September, this seems unlikely.

'No,' I say.

'He's a David Bowie tribute act,' he explains. 'Do you like David Bowie?'

I shrug as if to say, *Of course, doesn't everyone?*

'He's meant to be amazing. He has the voice down and even has two different-coloured eyes, although, to be fair, they're probably contact lenses. He's playing next Thursday at this place nearby and I wondered whether—'

'I have surgery every Friday morning,' I tell him, which is untrue. 'So I always get an early night on Thursdays. Sorry.'

'Oh, that's a pity,' he says. 'Then I guess I'll have to give my spare ticket to some other lucky girl.'

'I guess so,' I say, brushing past him as I try to achieve something that really shouldn't prove so difficult: gaining access to my own car.

'While we're talking,' he says, and I have to hand it to him: he's nothing if not determined. 'Your nephew mentioned to me that he was interested in television. I told him I'd invite him on set sometime on one condition. That you came too.'

He smiles at me, a dazzling smile, and I can tell that not only is he accustomed to women falling at his feet, he's absolutely convinced of his entitlement to such obeisance. He's good-looking in that boyish, non-threatening way that defines children's TV presenters, who generally look as if they were neutered at twelve, and I realize now that I've become not just a challenge, but an affront to his sense of self. He simply refuses to be rejected. I almost suspect that if I agreed to go out with him, he'd cancel at the last minute, just to prove a point. None of that matters right now, however, as I'm more concerned about what he's just said. For, after all, I'm not an aunt.

'My nephew,' I repeat slowly, half a question, half a statement.

'We met in the lift last week,' he tells me. 'At least, he said he was your nephew. I'm not wrong, am I?'

'No, you're not wrong,' I tell him. 'He did mention something about wanting to work in the arts. I just assumed he meant film or theatre, that's all. Not kids' TV.'

His jaw clenches a little at this, but I mean, come on. This is a man who spends an hour five days a week with his right arm stuck up the arse of a glove puppet called Biggles.

'I'll let him know,' I say, managing to insert myself into the driver's seat at last. 'I know he's busy with school at the moment, but maybe we can set something up somewhere down the line.'

'Only if you come too!' he repeats as I finally pull the door closed and turn on the engine. He remains where he is, watching me as I drive away.

I put this encounter out of my mind as I make my way towards Ramleigh Park. It's a pleasant, balmy evening, and the sun is starting to set. Halfway there, held up by some roadworks, I glance to my left and notice a group of teenagers gathered on the street. Two boys and a girl are playing Rock Paper Scissors and she apparently loses to both, because they whoop and holler and high-five each other. When the trio walks away, turning down a side street, I wonder where they're taking her, what consequence her loss involved, and only the aggressive beeping of the car behind me when the workmen allow us to drive on stops me from pulling in and following them to protect her.

When I reach the park, I find a parking space without

difficulty. A couple of pitches have been set aside for games of football. Both are occupied, the first by children aged around five or six, the second by the older boys.

I glance at my watch. It's seven fifteen, which suggests to me that they'll probably finish on the half-hour. I wish I'd brought a book and am about to turn the radio on when my phone rings, an unfamiliar number showing up on the screen. I press the red button to reject it, assuming it's some cold caller, but when it rings again a few moments later I decide to answer in case it's someone from work.

'Hello?' I say, waiting for the caller to speak, but there's only silence on the other end. 'Hello?' I repeat. 'Who's this?'

I'm about to hang up when a voice says, 'Is this Freya?' and immediately I know exactly who it is and end the call, flinging the phone away from me on to the floor of the passenger seat. I feel a burning sensation in the pit of my stomach, frightened that it might ring again, but, to my relief, it doesn't. When I finally build up the courage to retrieve it, I block the number on my text messaging service, on WhatsApp, and on the phone itself. How did this happen? I wonder, panicking. How does he have my number?

I consider going home. The combination of my encounter with Hugh and this unexpected communication has disturbed me. Perhaps the universe is conspiring to tell me that my plans for tonight are unwise. Despite the inevitable harassment, the prospect of a wine bar seems increasingly enticing, but before I can decide one way or the other, I notice that the football has come to an end and the teams are packing up their belongings. Immediately, I feel that intoxicating rush, that over-whelming thirst for revenge, that tells me I have no choice but to see this through.

The young kids leave first, whisked away by enraged fathers remonstrating with dejected five-year-olds over how they missed an open goal. The older boys follow. Some hang around in groups, some leave in pairs, shar-ing messages or pictures that have come through on their phones while they've been playing. Others begin walking home on their own. I scan them as they leave, waiting for the right boy to appear. I don't know who that is, but I will when I see him. It takes almost ten minutes before he turns on to the path. He's of average height for his age, and neither skinny nor muscular. He hasn't put on track-suit bottoms over his shorts, as some of the other boys have, and carries an enormous schoolbag on his back and a training bag over one shoulder. His blond hair needs cutting – he keeps brushing it out of his eyes – and one of his knees is covered in mud. He has AirPods in, and his head is moving slightly in time with whatever music he's listening to. Most importantly, he's alone. Per-haps he doesn't have any friends. It's always better if they don't.

I turn the engine on and allow him to walk a few hun-dred metres ahead. As he makes his way towards the traffic lights, I drive forward and pull up, waiting for him to reach me. When he does, I roll down the window on the passenger side and call out to him.

4

THE TWINS' NAMES WERE Arthur and Pascoe, trad-itional Cornish names, and to this day I don't know which of them came up with the idea of burying me alive, but, as they coexisted in a strangely symbiotic state, it's possible they devised the plan together through some unspoken telepathic power without either taking the lead.

When I think of that night, there are three things I recall above all else.

My frantic longing for water. The sound of the earth as they flung spadefuls down upon my improvised coffin. And my desperate need for air as I sucked what I could through the small breathing tube they had left me with. Only one of the four elements – fire – was missing that night, but its time would come.

Growing up in Norfolk with my grandmother, Hannah, I had been starved of the company of children my own age as she didn't allow me to socialize. Although she seemed ancient to me, Hannah was only thirty-two when I was born and thirty-three when my mother, Beth, moved to Cornwall, leaving me in her care. She preferred me to call her by her given name, insisting that 'Gran' made her sound like an old lady, just as my mother made me call her by hers because she didn't want people to think that she was old enough to have a child. Both had become pregnant when they were teenagers and, thinking this was the natural order of things, I assumed that I would be a mother myself at sixteen, but, thankfully, I realized that it would be cruel to bring a child into this world.

My first task when I got home from school every afternoon, regardless of the time of year, was to light the fire in the living room, a job I rather enjoyed, clearing out the ashes from the previous evening's blaze before sweeping the grate clean and re-laying it with crumpled-up pages from yesterday's newspaper, a few sticks of wood and pieces of coal, artfully arranged, and then taking a match to it all. I became proficient and could build the flames so they would burn all night.

For two months every summer, however, I was dispatched on the train to Cornwall to spend July and August with Beth, who threw her arms around me and wept when she collected me at the station, wrapping me in her cigarette-scented embrace, telling me how deeply she'd missed me and how much I had grown, but quickly becoming irritated by my presence. By the time we reached the small cottage she rented by the sea, the tears with which she'd greeted me had been replaced by eye-rolls and muttered asides if I asked too many questions, spoke too loudly, sang along with the radio, breathed too heavily, sniffed, coughed, scratched, opened the window, closed the window, did anything, in fact, to remind her of my existence. Instead of feeling welcome in her home or being overcompensated for her lack of maternal affection across the other ten months of the year, I always went to bed on my first night aware that she was counting down the days until I could be dispatched back to Norfolk.

With each passing summer, the cottage grew shabbier, while Beth grew skinnier and more wide-eyed. Her drinking and smoking, along with her habit of just picking at her food, made her increasingly gaunt, but this seemed to attract men, rather than turn them away. Every year, there was at least one new boyfriend for me to acquaint myself with, few of whom showed any interest in me, and in return I barely acknowledged their existence. There was little point, after all, in trying to build a relationship with someone who would be long gone by the time my next visit came around. There was a Derek, who sat on the sofa plucking impotently at the strings of his guitar. A Roger, who chewed his nails and spat the pieces across the room. A Dave, who told me that I'd better hope I grew into my face or no one would ever want to fuck me. A Nick, who was a Mormon, but, he insisted, a bad Mormon. A Chris, who took me for long walks along the beach with his enormous husky in tow. A Jonathan, who swore that he could have been the greatest actor of his generation, only other people were jealous of his talent and they'd ruined it for him. A Joe, who always had a can of cheap lager on the go. A Daisuke, whose family came from Hiroshima, 'where the bomb went off', but who had never travelled further east than Exmouth or further west than Penzance. A Gethin, who taught me how to spell and pronounce Llanfairpwllgwyngyllgogerychwyrndrobwllllantysiliogogogoch, the village in Anglesey where he had grown up. A Jasper, who read voraciously but rarely got past page fifty of any book. A Tom, whose conversation always seemed to return to the death of Princess Diana, which he insisted was a murder covered up by the Establishment. And these are just the ones that I remember. I didn't begrudge their presence in Beth's life. Each new addition, each throwaway, seemed as much part of who she was as the clothes she wore, the cheap make-up she applied every morning, or the roll-up cigarettes that always protruded from her right hand like a withered extra finger. She wouldn't have been Beth without any of them.

As uncomfortable as these visits could be, I enjoyed being in Cornwall. I liked the sunshine, the fresh air, and the screech of the seagulls in the morning. I liked the local curiosity shops and the winding lanes, some of which I ran quickly down, then struggled to ascend on the way home. But most of all I liked the beach, and that summer, the summer I was buried alive, I liked the fact that I made, or thought I made, some friends.

Beth's cottage was rented to her by a local man named Kitto Teague, who also owned the much larger property next door, having inherited both from his parents. The Teague home was probably five times the size of Beth's but had been in a state of bad repair for a number of years, and Kitto was in the process of making renovations. Enormous glass windows had been installed facing down towards the sea and the garden had been dug up and was due to be replanted. Beth's that-summer-boyfriend, Eli, who was friendlier to me than most of his predecessors, was site foreman and told me that Kitto was ploughing hundreds of thousands of pounds into the makeover.

'He wants it to look like one of them *Grand Designs* off the telly,' he told me. 'And it might do by the time we're finished.'

Beth liked to complain about the lorries that gathered outside, the delivery skips and large wooden boxes that brought new furniture in and took away the old, but there was nothing she could do about it. Her home was on Teague land, after all, and she lived in constant fear that her rent might be raised, or the cottage knocked down entirely to extend his property.

Aware of my interest in the house, Eli asked whether I wanted to see inside, and we waited until Mr Teague had gone into town for the day, when I followed him in, studying the shiny new stove and the granite marble of the kitchen island. Some of the workers lit cigarettes as soon as their employer had left and Eli shouted at them, saying they were causing a bloody fire hazard, and if they wanted to smoke, then they could bloody well do it down by the beach on their breaks. Even though he was younger than most of them, it impressed me to see how seriously he took his job and how attentive they were to his instructions.

Upstairs was more of a mess, but he explained the layout of the bedrooms and bathrooms and it was obvious that when all the work was finished it would be a beautiful home. I developed a fantasy that Eli would marry Beth, become my father, then divorce her and take me to live with him instead. He would build a home just like this one, only better, and I would never have to see either my mother or my grandmother again, but when I asked Beth whether she thought he might propose she just laughed and shook her head, saying she had no intentions of shackling herself to one man from here to eternity. Men, she told me, were like knickers. You needed to change them regularly.

We never talked about my real father. There was no point, as Hannah had already told me all I needed to know. That he was a lad from the year above Beth in school, a wrong 'un from a family of tinkers who were no better than they ought to be, and he'd just shrugged his shoulders when Beth told him that he'd got her up the spout, saying it was nothing to do with him if she was the town bike and how did she know it was his anyway? Half the school first eleven had had her.

'Which they hadn't,' she insisted. 'Not half, anyway.'

He left Norfolk before I was born and that was the end of that.

Before I met Arthur and Pascoe, I would spend my afternoons strolling up and down the beach, paddling in the water, and, on sunny days, changing into my swim-suit beneath a towel before swimming as far out as I dared, which wasn't far, as although I loved the water I had a terrible fear of sharks. (Hannah's favourite movie was *Jaws* and whenever it was on television she made me sit down to watch it with her, even though she knew that it gave me nightmares.)

Sometimes, I would observe other families on holidays, fathers, mothers and their children splashing around in the waves, building sandcastles, eating picnic lunches, and wished that I could be among them. I would have liked a brother or sister, someone for me to take care of, or someone who might take care of me, but when I asked Beth whether she would ever give me one, she said that she'd sorted that problem out years ago because being a mother was the hardest job in the world and she didn't intend doing it twice, even though, to my mind, she had barely done it once.

It was only a few days after Eli let me see inside the Teague mansion that I encountered the twins for the first time. I was walking down the path that led from the cottage to the beach and they were making their way simultaneously from the other side along a carefully constructed set of steps towards the end of their garden. I watched them carefully. Two boys. I would have preferred a boy and a girl, but I'd take what I could get.

'You're the Petrus girl, aren't you?' they said when our paths crossed, and their voices were like nothing I'd ever heard before. Posh, refined, condescending. Their family roots, I knew, were here in Cornwall, but they'd been brought up in Kensington, in West London, which Beth said was where the swanks lived.

'Them Teagues,' she told me, 'have more money than they know what to do with. He's a bigshot in some bank. Probably nicks it all from the vault.'

They stood tall, both of them, although they were still growing into their looks and needed haircuts. Almost in unison, they would blow air up from their lower lips to brush their fringes from their eyes, which was when I would see the scatter of pimples dotted across their foreheads. When they declared me 'the Petrus girl', it made me feel like they were talking to a member of staff, and, although I didn't like their tone, I longed for their company, anything to ease the isolation, so I said yes and told them they could call me Freya.

'He's Arthur,' said Pascoe, pointing towards his brother.

And, 'He's Pascoe,' replied Arthur, pointing back. 'Don't mix us up or we'll kill you.'

There was no chance of my doing that. They weren't identical and Arthur had a pronounced birthmark on his neck, just beneath the jawline, that looked a little like the map of the Thames that I saw at the start of *EastEnders*. I stared at it, wondering whether it was in fact a birthmark or he had been badly burned when he was younger. As I studied it his face reddened slightly, which only emphasized the deformity.

'How old are you?' I asked, and they told me. Fourteen.

'And you?'

'Twelve.'

'Just a kid,' said Arthur, laughing and shaking his head, and Pascoe joined in. I got the impression they were trying to mock me, but I *was* just a kid so I couldn't quite see how this could be considered an insult. What was wrong with being twelve? They'd been twelve themselves not so long before.

'Your house,' said Pascoe, nodding in the direction of Beth's cottage, 'belongs to us.'

'It's not mine,' I told him. 'I just stay with Beth for a couple of months every summer, that's all. I live in Norfolk.'

They rolled their eyes, as if this cast me even further down the proletarian ladder than they'd imagined. They asked about my father, and I told them, verbatim,

everything that Hannah had told me, even using her ter-
minology. *Wrong 'un. Tinkers. No better than they ought to
be. Up the spout.* I said that I'd seen their father come and
go over the last week but not their mother, and when I
asked whether she would be coming down to Cornwall
soon, their smiles faded. Arthur looked away, his glance
directed towards the water. Pascoe watched him for a
moment, appearing equally troubled.

'Mother died,' he said at last. 'Just after Christmas.
That's why we're here now, doing the bolthole up. Dad
says he needs a project.'

'What's a bolthole?' I asked, and Arthur pointed back
towards the house.

'That's a bolthole,' he told me.

I felt bad for them over the loss of their mum. The
mother of a girl in my class at school had died a few
months earlier in a car crash, along with the father of
another. Everyone had felt sorry for them at first, but
then it turned out they'd been having an affair, and, with
the casual malevolence of children, our sympathy dried
up instantly and the two grieving daughters, half-sisters
in adultery and tragedy, became sworn enemies.

'How did she die?' I asked, and, to my astonishment,
Pascoe told me that his father had murdered her, but that
the police hadn't found out because he was very clever
and they weren't supposed to tell anyone. Arthur remained
silent throughout this exchange but didn't seem surprised
by it. I didn't know whether Pascoe was having me on,
but I rather liked the idea of the story, so encouraged him
to tell me more. How did he kill her? I asked.

'Well, he didn't do it himself,' he told me. 'That would be asking for trouble. No, he hired someone. A trained assassin. Used to work for MI5 or MI6 or one of those places. Someone who knew exactly what he was doing.'

'But why?' I asked. 'Didn't he love her any more?'

'That's the thing,' he said. 'He loved her too much. So, when he found out that she was sleeping with someone else, he had to act. You do know what that means, don't you? Sleeping with someone else? Or are you too young yet?'

'I know what it means,' I declared haughtily, holding his gaze until he turned away. We'd started studying biology in school that year, and bodily parts, both male and female, their functions, what went where, and what happened when they did, had become the most common topic of conversation in the schoolyard as we offered both accurate and absurd explanations to each other.

'You can't tell anyone though,' said Arthur, squeezing my arm so tight that his fingermarks remained there for some time.

'If you do,' added Pascoe, 'then Father will murder you too.'

'And us.'

'All right,' I said, uncertain whether to believe them or not but unwilling to take the chance.

'You should be grateful we even told you,' he said, folding his arms and looking me up and down as if he was considering the price he might get for me on the open market. 'The only thing better than knowing a secret is having one of your own.'

5

BECAUSE THE BOY IS listening to music, I have to call out to him a few times before he notices me. He startles for a moment before removing his AirPods, his expression a little anxious, as if he's expecting me to reprimand him for some inadvertent transgression.

'Sorry,' I say, leaning across the passenger seat. 'You couldn't help me out, could you?'

He steps closer to the car now, glancing around but remaining silent. He has surprisingly large brown eyes and long eyelashes that put me in mind of a fawn.

'I'm a bit lost,' I explain, laughing to put him at ease. 'You don't know where Ramleigh Crescent is, do you?'

His face relaxes now. He hasn't done anything wrong. I'm just a woman who needs directions, that's all.

'Oh, right,' he says, looking down the street. 'I think you're pretty close, actually. Like . . . umm . . .' He points in the direction of a roundabout. 'You go down there, I think, and when you get to the traffic lights—'

'The first set?'

'Yes. Before the taxi rank.' He thinks about it, putting the thumb of his left hand to his mouth and holding it there as he deliberates. It reminds me of George biting his nails on the bench outside the hospital a few weeks earlier, a memory that sends a sharp burst of anxiety through me.

That phone call a few minutes ago.

'Is this Freya?'

'After that, I think you go left,' the boy continues. 'Although I'm not really sure. Do you have Google Maps?' His eyes flicker towards the dashboard of my Audi A8 and move hungrily across the various screens and the white leather interior.

'You look like a boy who's interested in cars,' I say, ignoring his question and smiling at him.

He nods and looks embarrassed, shuffling back on the pavement as he hitches his backpack up his shoulders.

'I couldn't ask an enormous favour, could I?'

'What?'

'You wouldn't jump in and direct me?' I ask. 'I hate to play the damsel in distress but I'm just really hopeless at things like this.'

He blinks, uncertain how to respond.

'Umm,' he says.

'I can barely find my own flat unless I'm standing in front of it,' I continue. 'And I've lived there for years.'

'Well, I suppose,' he mutters.

'You're a star,' I tell him, and, before he can change his mind, I reach over and open the passenger door. Still he doesn't move. He's probably been told from childhood that he should never get into cars with strangers, but it's not as if I'm some overweight middle-aged man trying to entice him into a Ford Fiesta with the promise of a burger and chips and a packet of Haribo afterwards. I'm an attractive thirty-six-year-old woman driving a sports car. I'm hardly a threat.

'I should probably go home,' he tells me. 'My mum . . .' he adds, trailing off.

'Do you live far?' I ask.

'Well, I get the bus.'

'Oh, buses are hopeless. They never come. And if they do, they break down or you can't get a seat. Tell you what. You help me find Ramleigh Crescent and then I'll drop you home once I know where it is. Deal?'

'Umm.'

Without waiting for an answer, I sit up straight in my seat and look ahead, as if we've agreed upon this plan, and although he remains tentative, he defaults to what I can only assume is his true nature: obedience. He's a good boy, and I like that. He'll do what he's told and cause no trouble. It takes a few moments, but at last he gets in, closes the door behind him, and before he can even put his seat belt on, I pull out, almost driving straight into the path of a passing van.

'Through the roundabout and all the way to the lights?' I ask.

'Yeah, I think so.'

We drive in silence at first and he keeps his backpack pressed firmly across his knees, as if it contains all his most precious possessions and not just his schoolbooks. His training bag is squashed on the floor around his feet.

'I'm Freya, by the way,' I tell him.

'Hi.'

I wait for him to offer his name, but he doesn't.

'And you?' I ask.

'Oh, sorry. Yeah. I'm Rufus.'

'That's an unusual name. I've never met a Rufus before.'

'I'm named after some singer my mum likes,' he tells me.

'Rufus Wainwright?'

'That's him.'

'Believe it or not, I heard him play live once,' I say, a total lie, but I'm aware of the album released from the performance. 'At Carnegie Hall in New York. He performed an entire concert that Judy Garland played there decades earlier.'

I hope this will inspire him to ask me something about it, just to get the conversation going, but no, total silence. He probably has no idea who Judy Garland is, so I mention *The Wizard of Oz* and he turns to me and smiles for the first time.

'Oh yeah,' he says. 'The Wicked Witch of the West.'

'That's the one.'

'She always scared me when I was a kid.'

I smile. He's still a kid, after all. And he was right to be scared of her.

'Well, it's nice to meet you, Rufus,' I say, accepting that I'm going to have to make all the running here. I nod towards his sports bag. 'You were playing football?'

'Trying to,' he tells me. 'I'm not very good.' He hesitates briefly, perhaps wanting to impress me. 'Although I did score a goal today.'

'Good for you!'

'An own goal,' he adds in a self-deprecating tone, and I burst out laughing.

'Well, a goal is a goal,' I say. 'You hit the back of the net. That's what counts.'

'Tell that to my teammates. I nearly got my head kicked in.'

We've reached the end of the road now and I turn left, as instructed. I know exactly where Ramleigh Crescent is and have absolutely no reason to visit it, but it's just off the main road that leads back to my own apartment building, which is all that matters. His phone rings and he takes it out of his pocket and looks at the screen.

'Mum,' he tells me.

'Are you not going to answer it?'

'No point. I know what it'll be about.'

'And what's that?'

'She'll be saying that she's going out for the night and has left me five quid on the table for a McDonald's.'

His answer couldn't be more perfect. No one's waiting for him at home.

'Is that a regular occurrence?' I ask, recalling how Hannah brought me up with a similarly cavalier attitude towards nutrition.

'Sometimes,' he says quietly, perhaps not wanting to sound disloyal to his mother.

'Can you even get a meal for five pounds?' I ask.

'Oh yes,' he replies, more confident now. He obviously knows his fast-food menus. 'Burger. Chips. Shake. Chicken nuggets.'

'Something for you to look forward to, then,' I say. 'Where do you live, anyway?'

He tells me. It's about a ten-minute drive east.

'Oh wait,' he says suddenly, pointing to my right as we pass Ramleigh Crescent. 'You've just gone past it.'

'That's fine,' I say. 'I don't need to go there right now. I'm looking at a house for sale tomorrow and wanted to be sure I knew where it was in case I got delayed on my way. I'll drop you home now if you like.'

'Thanks.'

'But, if you don't mind, can we just stop at mine first? It's on the way.'

He says nothing but starts fiddling with his fingers.

'I'm not holding you up, am I?' I ask.

'Well . . .'

'You probably have plans for the evening. Meeting your girlfriend or whatever.'

I glance towards him and watch as a blush spreads slowly from his neck towards his ears.

'No,' he says, awkwardly.

'You don't have a girlfriend?' I ask, doing my best to sound surprised.

'No.'

'A handsome boy like you? I thought you'd be fighting them off.'

He gives me a shy look that mixes pride with discomfort. His right leg has started to bounce up and down and he rests his hand on it, as if he's trying to keep it steady. His legs are slim with golden hairs sprinkled around the calves.

'Sorry, Rufus,' I say. 'Have I embarrassed you?'

'No,' he replies. 'It's just—'

'Just what?'

'My best friend, he has a girlfriend,' he says quickly, raising his voice a little, and I'm not sure why he's telling me this. Perhaps it's to make it sound as if he's connected to the world of sex in some way, if only at a one-step remove.

'Is she getting between you?'

'No,' he says, shaking his head. 'No, she's nice.'

'Do you mean that you like her too?'

'Well . . . not in that way, no.'

'All right,' I say. I would have preferred him to be a bit more negative about her, to tell me what a bitch she is, how she's destroying their friendship, but admire the fact that he's as loyal to his friend as he was to his mother. Again, a good boy. The best kind. The safest kind.

'I should probably get home,' he says.

'Hungry?'

'Yeah. And, you know, homework.'

'Of course,' I say. 'I'll just make that quick stop at mine and then we'll be on our way.'

'Actually,' he says, as the lights before us turn red. 'I can just get out here and jump on the bus.'

'Absolutely not,' I insist, prepared to press the child lock if necessary, although I'd rather not do something that might frighten him. 'A deal's a deal. I promised you a lift, and a lift is what you'll get.'

When we arrive at my building, I swing into the underground car park and the barriers lift when the camera

reads my licence plate. I can see that this impresses him.
Pulling into my spot, I turn the engine off.

'I'll wait here, will I?' he asks.

'No, come upstairs. It can be dangerous sitting in car
parks on your own. You never know who might come
along and, I don't know, try to molest you or something.'
I laugh and he looks down at his feet. I notice his eyes
open wide as if he's holding some complicated internal
conversation with himself. 'It'll only take a few minutes.
I'll show you where I live. A famous footballer used to
live in my apartment, you know.'

He has no choice, because I offer him none, and also
because I'm an adult and he's still, technically, a child. I
get out of the car and stand there, waiting for him to
exit too, and eventually he does. Happily, there's no one
else nearby. I have a dread of Hugh Winley appearing
suddenly out of the darkness, like Deep Throat in *All
the President's Men*, still demanding that I go on a date
with him.

We make our way towards the lift and I inhale the universal scent of teenage boy: perspiration, anxiety and
Lynx. Closing my eyes as we ascend towards the twelfth
floor, I breathe carefully, as I always do when I'm trapped
in enclosed spaces. I can tell from Rufus's expression that
he has no idea what he's doing here and is growing
increasingly uncertain. When I look up towards the rising
numbers, I feel his gaze travelling to the opened button
on my blouse, where a hint of red bra peeps out from
beneath the white. I reach down, as if to scratch an itch,
and allow another button to pop open, pretending I don't

know that it has, and he exhales a little louder before covering it up with a cough.

I lead him towards my apartment and unlock the door, standing back to allow him to enter first. The table lamp I left on earlier offers the perfect glow against the evening light that seeps in through the windows and he steps inside, looking around.

'This is really nice,' he tells me, his eyes widening. He wanders over to the other side of the room, where glass doors open on to a balcony that faces an identical building opposite.

'Thanks,' I say. 'Do you like music?'

'Umm, I guess.'

I tell Siri to play a song that relaxes me, a ballad, and he listens for a moment.

'I'm learning piano,' he tells me.

'Oh yes? And how's that going?'

'It's OK,' he replies, blushing again, as if he already regrets revealing any detail about his life. I can tell that he wants to talk to me, but he's a nervous, anxious fourteen-year-old boy, and every time he says something, he immediately regrets it. I leave him alone for a moment, going to the bedroom to retrieve the purse I deliberately left on my dressing table earlier.

'Sorry,' I say, holding it in the air when I return. 'I forgot this, and I'm nearly out of petrol. Might have to stop at a garage on the way.'

Another lie, of course. I filled the tank yesterday.

'It's fine,' he says. 'But I should probably get home now.'

'Why? No one's expecting you, are they?'

He looks at me and blinks a few times.

'You said your mother's going out.'

'I know, but—'

'No, you're right. I've already taken up enough of your time. Although I am a bit thirsty. I might just grab a quick drink. Would you like one?'

He looks around the room.

'Umm.'

'I'm pretty sure I have a Coke in the fridge,' I tell him. 'Would you like a Coke?'

'Umm.'

I don't go to the fridge just yet. Instead, I walk towards him. His skin is remarkably clear. I can tell that he's the sort of boy who isn't going to suffer acne and wonder what he'll look like when he's older. Right now, he's neither a boy nor a proper teenager. His face has a blankness to it that could develop into anything. He could be one of those innocent, asexual boys larking around naked in a Henry Scott Tuke painting or a tattooed thug living on a council estate and dealing drugs to children. But while he's blameless now, almost angelic, it's only a matter of time before he matures and not only recognizes his power to destroy girls in pursuit of what he wants but acts upon it. Right now, as I stand before him, some innocent twelve-year-old girl is lying on her bed not far from here, plaiting the hair of her dolls, looking up at the fairy lights that brighten her room or the luminous stars on her ceiling, completely oblivious to the fact that, one day, she'll be one of his victims.

'Let me get you that Coke,' I say.

FIRE

I make my way into the kitchen and take the can from the fridge, shaking it vigorously before returning to the living room and handing it to him. He looks at it as if there's nothing he wants less, but it's in his hands now so he has no choice but to open it. When he does, it explodes, of course, and his football shirt is soaked within seconds. He cries out in dismay before dropping it on a side table, where it fizzes over the top, then looks at me in mortification.

'I'm so sorry,' he says, as if it's his fault that this has happened and not mine.

'Don't worry,' I say, stepping towards him. 'Accidents happen. But look at you, you're drenched!' He peels the polyester fabric away from his skin. 'You can't wear it home like that. Take it off and I'll put it on a quick wash and dry for you. It won't take long.'

His expression changes to one of pure terror. The last thing he wants to do is remove his shirt.

'It's OK,' he says.

'Take it off,' I insist, reaching down and lifting it from its base, like a mother undressing a toddler, before dragging it higher. He lifts his arms and I pull it up, bringing it into the kitchen, where I simply toss it on the floor. I have no intention of doing his laundry; I'm not his servant. When I return, he's wrapped his arms around his pale, white chest and is looking down at the floor.

I come closer.

'Look at you. All sticky.' I press my index finger to his sternum before drawing it slowly down towards his navel. 'You know what you need?'

'What?' he whispers, his voice cracking in a single syllable.

'A shower.'

'I'm fine,' he tells me, shaking his head quickly.

'You're not fine,' I reply. 'What kind of person would I be if I sent you home like this? Some kind of monster. Just like the Wicked Witch of the West.' I step even closer to him now, and our eyes meet. I can feel his tension, his fear, his desire, his confusion. It's a combination that intoxicates me. I try to recall the name of the child I treated a few weeks ago, named after the Norse god of vengeance, but it escapes me for the moment.

I lower my voice, almost whispering.

'You're very shy, aren't you, Rufus?' I say. 'Boys your age are usually so overconfident. It's refreshing to meet one who isn't.'

Gently, I place the flat of my right hand against his chest.

Vidar, that was it. *Vidar.*

'Don't be nervous,' I say, taking his hand now as I lead him towards the bathroom. 'You can trust me.'

6

It's not often that I find myself completely surprised, but when Aaron knocks on my office door and asks whether we might go for a drink together some evening, I'm so astonished that it takes me a moment to respond.

'A drink?' I ask, turning away from my computer screen to give him my full attention. I don't for a moment think he's asking me on a date – that would be utterly bizarre – but I'm puzzled why he'd think I'd want to socialize with him, considering how abruptly I've treated him since his rotation began.

'Yes,' he says. 'If you're busy, I totally understand. It's just that we only ever speak here, and I'd be grateful for an opportunity to talk in a less formal atmosphere. About my career.'

I'd like to say no, to tell him that the moment I walk out the front doors in the evening, that's it, my duties have come to an end, but I need to be seen to be helpful to junior doctors; after all, they submit evaluations on us, just as we do on them. And so, fine, I tell him, somewhat grudgingly, suggesting Saturday, which will at least break up an otherwise empty weekend for me and disrupt a busy one for him.

On Friday, he emails the name of a bar in town, and when I arrive, deliberately late, I'm rather impressed to see the effort he's made. He's wearing a pair of grey jeans, paired with a crisp white shirt, and a sturdy pair of boots that matches his belt, and a brown leather jacket rests on the banquette beside him. He smells good too; colognes and perfumes are banned in the hospital but whatever he's sprayed himself with this evening offers a pleasant scent of wood and vanilla. Has he got dressed up just for me? I wonder.

'Dr Petrus,' he says, leaning forward, as if to kiss my cheek, but quickly realizing that this would be an unwise move. 'Thank you for coming.'

'You can call me Freya,' I tell him. 'We're not in work now.'

'Freya,' he repeats, bowing his head briefly, like I'm a member of the royal family and he's greeting me on one of my engagements. 'What can I get you to drink?'

I ask for a vodka and cranberry and, while he's gone, I glance around the bar. It's almost full, with most tables populated by couples or foursomes, friends on a night out. It feels strange to be in their company. Any one of them might look towards Aaron and me and assume that we're in a relationship too, and while I have no ambitions in that regard, and would shut down any advances on his part, it's not unpleasant to feel like a normal member of society for a change. This is how my life might have been, I think, had it not been for the Teagues.

When he returns with my drink and a fresh beer for him, we move seamlessly into small talk. A famous rock star has died earlier in the day and we discuss her life and career. A scandal involving a prominent banker is growing and he confides in me that the disgraced woman is his mother's first cousin. There's some mention of a trip to Amsterdam that he's looking forward to. And then, rather unexpectedly, he tells me this:

'You know, I applied to the hospital specifically because I wanted to work with you.'

'Really?' I say, raising an eyebrow. In our profession, there are plenty of famous doctors, but I'm not one of them. Burns, the whole field of plastics in general, doesn't usually attract much attention, unlike the more glamorous arenas of brain and heart, which tend to draw physicians blessed in the former but lacking in the latter. 'Why?'

'Because you're the person who made me want to be a doctor.'

I reach for my glass and wonder whether he's just flattering me with an eye to advancement. For a moment, my eyes focus on his hands. He has the fingers of a surgeon, I think. Bony. Steady. Repulsive.

'I don't understand,' I say.

'The Rozelli Programme,' he says, and I groan, as there are few phrases that I dread as much as this. The initiative is one that the hospital introduced more than a decade earlier and involves medical professionals visiting local schools and universities with the hope of encouraging students to pursue careers in the NHS. I've been forced to take part on numerous occasions and, while I do what I can to get the pupils enthused, it's not something I enjoy. 'You gave a talk to our year when we were doing our GCSEs,' he continues. 'You told us about patients you'd helped and showed slides of people who'd been trapped in fires. How you'd helped them get back to some meaningful form of life. Most of my friends found it a bit upsetting, but not me. I found it inspiring. I found *you* inspiring.'

'Well, that's good to hear,' I tell him, pleased that whatever I said encouraged him in some way. 'To be honest, I've never felt very confident when it comes to public speaking. But it's become something of a requirement for surgeons and senior consultants. The Rozelli Foundation pumps a lot of money into the hospital, but they do make us dance for it.'

'You spoke so passionately about what you do,' he continues. 'I don't want to sound melodramatic, but that day changed my life.'

I can't help but smile. I'm not usually susceptible to flattery, but he seems sincere. Whatever my allergy is to him, I let it go for now.

'Thank you, Aaron,' I say. 'That's kind of you to say.' I pause and offer a small concession. 'I know I'm not always the easiest person to work with, but—'

'Your focus is on your patients,' he says, cutting me off. 'I know that. And I'm just some know-nothing intern getting in your way. I'd be a cunt too if I was you.'

I blink, uncertain I've heard him right over the noise of the bar.

'I'm sorry?' I ask. 'What did you just say?'

'I said I'd be curt too if I was you.'

I remain silent for a moment, examining his face for any sign of disrespect, but he seems sincere enough.

'You're a good doctor,' I tell him eventually, even though I don't have any strong feelings on the subject one way or the other. 'You have a good career in front of you.'

We move on to other subjects. We talk about Louise and how she'll be missed when she retires in a few weeks' time. He tells me about a thriller he's reading that he thinks I might enjoy featuring a murderous paediatrician as its central character. I mention a film I've heard good things about and he says that he hasn't been to the cinema in more than a year. The last time he went, he witnessed a road traffic accident on the way home and ended up testifying in court as a witness, an experience he found strangely exhilarating.

'Actually, I know that feeling,' I tell him, ordering fresh drinks from a passing lounge girl. She glances at Aaron appreciatively, offering him a flirtatious smile, and to my surprise I feel like scratching her eyes out. 'I served on a jury once. I would have preferred to get out of it, but in the end it turned out to be quite interesting.'

'Really?' he asks. 'What kind of a case was it?'

'Rape.'

He pulls a face.

'That must have been difficult,' he says.

'Why?'

'Well, as a woman . . .' He drifts off, perhaps sensing that, considering the times we live in, he's veering into dangerous territory.

'You're assuming it was a woman who was raped,' I say.

'That's true. Am I wrong?'

'No, but you shouldn't assume.'

'You're right.'

'Are you a football fan?' I ask.

He nods.

'Then you might remember Evan Keogh and Robbie Wolverton.'

'I do,' he says. 'One of them raped a girl and the other filmed it. They played for my team. My old team, I mean. I walked away after that.'

'They both swore that the encounter had been consensual, and we believed them. We found them not guilty. It's not something I'm particularly proud of. We didn't feel that the prosecution had proved their case beyond a reasonable doubt, so we found for the defence.'

'I read somewhere that forty thousand women report a rape to the police every year.'

'Actually, it's closer to seventy thousand.'

'And you didn't feel like . . . I don't know . . . making an example of them?'

'No. The truth and the facts don't always tally. But, of course, it didn't end there. A couple of years later, Keogh confessed. Went to the police and admitted everything. He even handed over the video evidence. In a way, you have to admire him for finally coming clean.'

'Maybe his conscience got to him,' suggests Aaron.

'Maybe,' I agree. 'It would be so much easier to go through life if you didn't have one, don't you think?'

'No,' he says, his immediate and emphatic reply

surprising me, even though this was just a throwaway comment on my part. 'I think it would be horrific.'

'Anyway, they were re-arrested, re-tried, and they had no choice but to plead guilty. Wolverton's still in jail. He'll be there for another five years.'

'And Keogh killed himself,' says Aaron.

'Well, he was found dead in his cell. It was all a bit Jeffrey Epstein, if you ask me. It's hard to know what to believe.'

We talk about this a little more, then change the subject again. I want to know more about him. I ask whether he has a girlfriend and he tells me that he does.

'What's her name?'

'Rebecca,' he replies.

'Is she studying medicine too?'

'No,' he says, shaking his head. 'She's training to be a pilot.'

I know I shouldn't be surprised by this, but I am. It's still a relatively unusual career path for a woman.

'And how long have you been together?'

'Almost two years now.'

For some inexplicable reason, I feel jealous.

'How about you?' he asks. 'Do you have a partner?'

His use of the word 'partner' makes me think that he's hedging his bets so as not to offend me.

'I do,' I lie.

'And their name?'

Their. He's still covering himself.

'Eli,' I say.

'And what does he do?'

'He's a SPAD.'

'A what?'

'A SPAD,' I say. 'You don't know what a SPAD is?'

He shakes his head, orders more drinks. I ask for a large this time.

'No,' he says. 'It sounds like something to do with gardening.'

'That's a spade, you moron,' I reply, teasing him and touching him on the upper arm. 'A SPAD is a special adviser. He reports to the Chancellor of the Exchequer, in fact.'

'That's pretty cool,' says Aaron, impressed.

'Cooler than being a surgeon?'

'No, nothing is that cool. Not even being a pilot.'

'Good boy,' I say, patting him on the hand now, and, instead of laughing along with me, he appears annoyed by the phrase, which I only meant as a joke, and pulls his hand away.

'So have you met the prime minister?' he asks.

I tell him that I have. That we're quite friendly, in fact. That I gave him a book for Christmas and he gave me a scented candle. I enjoy building this fantasy life, just as I enjoyed creating Jesse, the imaginary boyfriend of my twenties. The more alcohol that enters my bloodstream, the better I get at lying, or at least I think I do. Perhaps I should have been a novelist. I could have spent every day inventing lives much more interesting than my own.

'I'm sorry if I've been hard on you, Aaron,' I say at last, because the evening has gone much better than I expected and, to my surprise, I find that I've rather enjoyed it. 'But you must recognize the importance of our work. A hospital isn't a social club, you know? We're not there to make friends. Our sole responsibility is towards our patients. So, if I've been short with you from time to time, please don't take it personally. It just means that I have to put all my attention where it's most needed. It will toughen you up.'

'I'm tougher than you think,' he tells me. 'But can I ask, why did you choose burns?'

'I'm sorry?'

'Of all the disciplines. Why burns?'

No one has ever asked me this before. I have no parents. I have no siblings. I have no friends. I'm entirely alone in the world, so my choices have always been my own and unquestioned. I consider the question carefully, wanting to give him an honest answer.

'Because people turn away,' I say at last.

He frowns. It's obvious he doesn't understand what I mean.

'If you have cancer,' I explain, 'everyone is on your side. They'll wear ribbons and run marathons to raise money for your treatment. You're sanctified for developing a disease over which you have no control. If you have Alzheimer's, your family has to figure out how to look after you while secretly hoping you'll have made plans for a one-way trip to Switzerland. As humans, from the moment we reach puberty, we search for beauty. We do it in our daily lives, whether we're looking at someone we want to fuck or someone we want to fuck us. But beauty is meaningless. It's nothing more than the manner in which the skin is formed over the skull. And the skull is nothing more than the way the bones have been formed in the womb. None of it means anything. Beautiful people have so many advantages. You're a good-looking guy. I know I'm an attractive woman. But have you ever wondered what it would be like to be blessed with such extraordinary beauty that, when you walk into a bar, every head turns in your direction?'

'I'm sure that happens with you,' he says. 'I'm not trying to be creepy, but—'

'No, I get it. And yes, it does. Sometimes. But that will come to an end soon. The elements destroy everything. Think of water. When someone drowns, and their body floats back to shore, their features are so bloated it can be difficult to identify them. Think of earth. When a body is buried, it starts to decompose immediately. Think of air. If we're deprived of it for even a few minutes, we die. Then think of fire. When someone's physical appearance is damaged by burns, we turn away, repulsed. We don't want to know.'

An old Hot Chocolate song sounds over the speakers, one I haven't heard in many, many years. 'It Started With A Kiss'. I glance at Aaron. For some inexplicable reason, he's laughing a little. Do I want to kiss him? I *should* want to kiss him. So why don't I? He's not exactly age appropriate, but he's not entirely age inappropriate either. No one would bat an eyelid.

My mind drifts back to Cornwall, to Arthur and Pascoe, and to the night they buried me alive. I could tell him this story. I could tell him the real reason that I chose burns as my speciality. I could tell him everything about my life, about who I am, about what I do, and see how he reacts. But I'm not stupid. Nor am I drunk enough to reveal the worst of myself to this relative stranger. I've sat through a trial once and have no desire to do so again.

'Twelve thousand,' says Aaron after a lengthy silence, apparently apropos of nothing.

'I'm sorry?' I say.

'Twelve thousand,' he repeats. 'That's how many men report being sexually assaulted in the UK every year. We forgot to mention them when we were talking about rape figures earlier.'

He's right too. In some ways, it doesn't surprise me that he knows the exact statistics for men but underestimated the number for women by almost fifty per cent. But it disappoints me.

And just when I was beginning to think well of him too.

7

WHETHER OR NOT ARTHUR and Pascoe's father had, in fact, murdered their mother would forever remain a mystery to me for I never asked them about it again.

When I spoke to Beth about her landlord, she simply shrugged her shoulders, saying that she didn't know him well and that he only came by occasionally to make sure she was keeping the place in good repair. Eli was equally unhelpful, telling me that all he'd ever discussed with Kitto Teague were his plans for the renovation and as soon as the place was finished he'd be glad to move on, as Teague was a tight-fisted London sod who condescended to the locals and never got his round in.

While the house's overhaul intrigued me, I was more interested in the great pit being dug towards the rear of the mansion, looking down on to the beach, into which, eventually, a swimming pool would be installed. It was intended to be the final construction job; until then, it was being used to dispose of all the building site's detritus, and every Tuesday morning an enormous lorry came by to empty it.

'Why do you need a pool when you live so close to the sea?' I asked the twins, leaning over the side one after-noon and looking down. There was no rain that summer and the base was a rich shade of blackish brown, a mix-ture of cracked earth and displaced sand that blew in overnight from the coastline.

'Because we're rich,' said Arthur. 'And rich people have pools.'

Having never known any rich people, I accepted this as perfectly reasonable. Beth lived from hand to mouth, working in a pub most evenings and cleaning holiday homes during the season, while, back in Norfolk, Hannah held down three jobs, a café in the mornings, a bar at night, and a fast-food restaurant on Saturday evenings, although she still never seemed to have any money.

I tried to picture what it might look like when it was filled with water, imagining the sides tiled in bright green with a mural of cartoon fish spread across the base. I wondered whether the Teagues might allow me to swim in it the following summer when I returned or whether they would keep it just for themselves.

My relationship with Arthur and Pascoe developed slowly over those first weeks, and although we spent most of our time together, I found their company as irritating as it was addictive. They liked to lord over me the fact that they were fourteen while I was only twelve, infer-ring that they knew so much more about the world than me, although I suspected, being poor, that I understood it a lot better than they did. Sometimes they became shy, particularly at the beach, when I slipped beneath a towel to change into my swimsuit. Then I would catch them watching me, their faces growing red when I ordered them to turn away, and they would be less confident until we were all dressed again, at which point they would reassert their dominance.

At other times, they could be aggressive, although never with each other, pushing me roughly or dragging me to the ground in a game of wrestling, covering my body with theirs, their hands mauling every part of my skin that was available to them. I would give back as good as they gave until, finally, they would jump away from me in a sudden rush, looking awkward and confused as they tugged at the crotch of their shorts.

I had only known one other set of twins before, two girls in my class in school. They were as different as diamonds and dust and didn't seem to like each other very much, let alone want to spend any time together, sitting far apart in the classroom and socializing with different groups of friends. In the two months I spent with Arthur and Pascoe, however, I don't think I ever saw either of them alone.

Once, they brought me upstairs in their house while their father was out to show me their makeshift bedroom, which contained a double bed that they slept in together. The walls were entirely bare, not a book, toy or photograph in sight.

'What do you think of that?' asked Arthur, giving me a sordid look that I was too young to understand. I didn't think anything of it, I told him. What was I supposed to think? It was just a bedroom. Everyone had one.

JOHN BOYNE

'It's only for now,' explained Pascoe. 'When the house is finished, we'll have beds of our own.'

'Although we'll still share a room,' insisted Arthur.

'Definitely,' replied his brother.

Sometimes, when we were rambling around the dunes, they would grow tired of my company, almost forgetting that I was there, and I might slip behind, happy to be on my own for a while. When I'd eventually catch up with them, I would discover them walking hand in hand, something I had never seen two boys do before, or sitting by the rocks, staring out to sea, one boy's head resting on the other's shoulder. If one ran off to pee, the other went with him and, at first, I thought it was because he didn't want to be left alone with me, but in time I started to realize that they simply couldn't bear to be apart. Their need to touch each other regularly, even if it was just a slap on the back or an arm around the other, struck me as strange but affectionate.

Then, one day, they told me about the caves that had been eroded into the rocks of Cornwall over centuries.

'Smugglers used them hundreds of years ago,' explained Pascoe. 'They came from France, bringing gold, diamonds and whisky with them. They had a whole crew of accomplices around the coastline so they could distribute everything and make their fortunes. But they hid lots of stuff in the caves too in case they got caught, and sometimes they forgot about it or died or drowned and it was left behind. Half these caves have hidden treasure in them if you look hard enough. It might be buried deep under the sand, or in the nooks and crannies, but it's there. When we were down here at Easter, I found a gold necklace.'

I raised an eyebrow, unconvinced. It sounded like something they'd read in a book. They seemed offended by my disbelief.

'We'll show you,' they said, and we walked down the hills together, descending carefully as the stone beneath our feet was sharp and unforgiving.

'You can only come here at low tide,' said Arthur. 'If you came in the evening, it wouldn't be long until the caves filled with water and you'd drown.'

The idea of this made me uncertain whether I wanted to risk entering, just in case the tide came in early, but the sun was still high in the sky and the waves were placid so there seemed little risk. Still, something about the place reeked of danger, and my reluctance must have been obvious.

'Come on,' said Pascoe, reaching out and trying to drag me forward. 'Don't be a girl.'

'But I am a girl,' I told him.

'That's no reason to act like one,' said Arthur. 'Take our hands,' he said, looking at his brother, who walked back and stood on the other side of me. 'The whole point of coming here is to explore it together.'

I was intrigued, certainly, and, unwilling to be bested by them, I finally agreed. Inside, it was brighter than I had expected, the daylight sparking into the passageway and bouncing off the glossy, sea-sprayed rocks. Tunnels led left and right with the occasional hollow allowing light to spill through from the surface. I thought of Ali Baba and the Forty Thieves and wondered whether, when I turned a corner, I might be confronted by chests filled with gold. I could fill my pockets, I told myself, and bring it all back to Hannah and Beth. Or, better still, I could run away with it and never have to see either of them again.

As we ventured further into the interior, I began to worry that we'd taken so many turns we might be unable to retrace our steps. I didn't want to appear frightened, however, so was relieved when Arthur said, 'We can stop here, this is the best place.'

Looking ahead, I saw a rough wall of black stone and in front of it an area filled with sand and tiny stones, the accumulation of centuries of night waves eroding the rocks here before breaking them down into pebbles. I was glad to have reached the end and turned around, ready to return, when Arthur stepped in front of me, blocking my way, as Pascoe took up position behind.

'Not yet,' said Arthur, looking me up and down, and the pupils of his eyes seemed to grow larger as he reached out to stroke my bare arm. 'There's a game we like to play, but we only play it here. Where no one can see us.'

'What kind of game?' I asked.

'A fun game.'

'Aren't all games fun? Isn't that the point?'

Arthur and Pascoe looked at each other. They obviously hadn't expected me to be quite so provocative.

'They're meant to be,' agreed Arthur. 'But this one is more fun than anything we've played before. And it'll be even better with a girl.'

He reached out and took my hand, pressing it to the

crotch of his shorts, and when I didn't immediately remove it, he smiled and glanced towards his brother, who was watching us intently.

Looking back, I don't think I told him to stop; not that first time, anyway. It was exciting and, recalling all those schoolyard conversations, I wanted to see what it was like. It wasn't what I expected. From what little I understood, I thought it was supposed to be enjoyable for both people, but it wasn't enjoyable for me. I felt like a piece of meat, lying on the ground, while Arthur did what he wanted to it. He didn't even look me in the eye. When he was finished, however, which was only two or three minutes later, Pascoe started to unbuckle the belt on his shorts, and this time I did say no.

'That's not fair!' he cried. 'You can't do it with Arthur and not with me.'

'I can,' I said, pulling myself to my feet a little unsteadily. I wanted to run into the water and wash myself. I felt grubby and dirty, embarrassed by what had happened. My natural twelve-year-old curiosity had given way to immediate shame.

'No!' insisted Arthur. 'He's my brother. If I get to do it, then he does too.'

I glanced behind me. There were several tunnels leading from where we were and I wasn't sure which one would take me back to the beach and which would lead me further into an inescapable labyrinth.

'I'm going home,' I said, turning away, but Pascoe ran ahead, cutting me off.

'It's my turn!' he shouted. 'You said we could both do it!'

'I didn't!' I cried, because I'd said no such thing. 'I can't, anyway. It hurt.'

'Freya,' said Arthur patiently. 'Do you know what a tease is?'

I shook my head.

'It's when a girl leads a boy on,' he explained, 'but then won't go all the way. It's the worst thing any girl can do.'

'It's even worse than murdering someone,' agreed Pascoe.

'But I don't want to,' I repeated, starting to cry now, because, while I may have been complicit in what had taken place with Arthur, I knew that I didn't want to do it again. With anyone. For a long time.

Seeing that I wasn't going to change my mind, Arthur pushed me to the ground and pulled my arms back, pinning them down. The moment violence took over, my brain seemed to disassociate itself from my body. A part of me thought that one of them would take a rock and bash my brains in, killing me like Kitto Teague had supposedly killed their mother, if I didn't give in. And so I lay there and he did what he wanted to do.

Every day over the next month, they would collect me after lunch and we would make our way to the caves together, rarely talking now, and the same thing would happen. Looking back, I don't understand why I allowed it to continue. I didn't enjoy it, but I was worried that they would abandon me. I was twelve and desperately lonely. Thanks to Hannah's insistence on my being her unpaid servant, I'd never been allowed to have a friend, let alone two of them. Perhaps this, I told myself, is what good girls did for their friends.

Eventually, however, I decided that I'd had enough. Beth didn't notice my change of mood, but Eli did and asked me about it. I wanted to confide in him but worried that if he knew the things I'd been doing, then he would want to do them with me too. And he was so much bigger and stronger than the twins that the idea was too frightening for me even to contemplate.

When I told the boys that I wouldn't go to the caves with them any more, they said I had no choice, that the game only ended at the end of the holiday.

'No,' I insisted. 'It's not going to happen again.'

'And what makes you so sure of that?' asked Pascoe.

'Because,' I said, 'if you make me do it again, I'll tell.'

This unnerved them, and I felt I had regained some power. After this, I didn't see them for three days and, despite myself, felt even lonelier than ever, wondering whether I had made a mistake. When they finally called at the cottage again late one night, Beth was out as usual and I was already preparing for bed.

'We're sorry,' said Arthur, holding a bunch of flowers in his hands, and there was something about his forlorn expression that made me think that he really was.

'Really sorry,' added Pascoe.

'We still want to be friends.'

I looked from one boy to the other and felt a surge of gratitude towards them. They were company. And I longed for company. It only took me a moment to say that I forgave them.

'There's something we want to show you,' said Pascoe, and I shook my head and said that whatever it was, it would have to wait until the next day. I was too tired.

'No, this is too good to miss,' said Arthur. 'It's only up by the swimming-pool pit.'

'What is it?' I asked, intrigued.

'You have to see it for yourself,' he told me, and, not wanting to fall out with them again, I agreed, putting on some warmer clothes and allowing them to lead the way.

The pit looked much the same as it always did. The lorry had come a few days earlier so it was once again half full of paint cans, ripped cardboard and enormous empty boxes. Arthur and Pascoe were standing by what looked to be a wooden chest, and from the words on the side I could tell that it must have held some of the latest furniture to arrive.

'Come down,' they insisted, and when Arthur held out a hand for me, I took it and joined them. They opened the lid of the chest and we all looked inside. It was empty. Arthur climbed in, and he didn't have to squeeze up too much to fit; it was the perfect size for a boy his age. I stared down, wondering why he was bothering. When he clambered out again, Pascoe took a turn and lay down too, his arms crossed across his chest, as if he was lying in a coffin. He closed his eyes, waited a few moments, then slowly sat up, speaking like Dracula.

'*I want to drink your blood.*'

I rolled my eyes. It seemed strange to me that they'd dragged me all the way here just to look at an empty box.

'Your turn,' said Arthur, turning to me when his brother got out, and I shook my head.

'No, thanks,' I said.

'You scared?'

I wasn't. I just couldn't see the point of climbing into a box only to climb out again.

'She's scared,' said Arthur, turning to his brother, who nodded.

'It's because she's a girl,' agreed Pascoe, and I sighed and said fine, I'd do it. I climbed inside and lay down on my back, just as Pascoe had done, and looked up at them. In the sky was a full moon and it caught my eye as I stared at the grey shapes dotted across it, which I decided were continents, and on one of those continents were countries, and in one of those countries was a city, and in that city were houses, and my father lived in one of those houses and he wasn't a wrong 'un at all, but was kind and lonely and missed me.

'Happy?' I asked, but instead of answering, they pulled the lid of the box over, shutting it tight. Immediately, everything went black. Shocked, I didn't even have the strength of mind to push it back up, and a hammering began from outside. To my horror, I realized that they were nailing it closed. After a moment, I found my voice and started banging at the makeshift ceiling, calling their names, begging to be set free.

'You need to think about your behaviour,' said Arthur casually, and then I heard the sound of earth from the pit being thrown on top of my coffin. 'Don't worry, you'll still be able to breathe. We've left a hole free above you and we'll send a tube down. But you'll be in there for a while, so you might as well get used to it.'

I screamed and continued to push at the roof as more soil landed and, even though I knew the chest was already at the base of the pit, I imagined the scene from outside, the entire quarry being filled with soil and me disappearing for ever beneath it. I banged and banged, growing more terrified than I had ever been in my life before. This was it, I told myself. This was how I was going to die.

Buried alive.

8

I T'S BEEN A FEW weeks since my evening with Rufus, which turned out to be far more troubling than my usual encounters.

He was clearly alarmed when I led him into the bathroom, even more so when I turned the shower on, but when I took my blouse off, he emitted some strange, petrified sound that blended confusion, desire and terror into one. I've experienced similar reactions before, of course. Among their friends, most of these boys act as if they could put Casanova to shame, but in reality they're all completely terrified of women.

When we made it to the bedroom, he lay beneath me with such a frightened expression on his face that anyone would think I was forcing myself upon him, and when he whispered, 'Please don't hurt me,' I was this close to telling him to gather his things and leave. His body reacted as it should, however, and somehow we got through it. When it was over, he slipped out from beneath me and slunk to the floor, staring down at the carpet.

I left him to it, returning to the bathroom to clean up, and when I emerged, he'd at least had the dignity to drag himself to his feet and was sitting on the side of the bed, wearing his football shorts and Coke-stained T-shirt again, but still barefoot. Only now did he turn to look at me, rearing back a little as if I posed some sort of threat.

'Why did you do that to me?' he whispered.

'Why did I do what?'

'What you just did.'

I watched as he reached for his socks, slowly pulling them on, and decided to ignore his question.

'You should probably leave now,' I told him, which was when I realized that he was drying tears from his cheeks. 'Why are you crying?' I asked. 'If anyone should be upset here, it's me.'

He looked at me and frowned, then tried to put his runners on but struggled with this rather basic task, possibly because his hands were shaking so much.

'You're putting them on the wrong feet,' I said, going over to help him, but he pulled away.

'Don't touch me!' he shouted, so loudly that I jumped back.

'Jesus, fine,' I said, holding my hands in the air. 'But the left runner goes on the left foot and the right runner goes on the right. It's not rocket science.'

The tears came faster now, and he ran the insides of his elbows across his eyes to wipe them dry.

'You can stop blubbing,' I said. 'I'm not going to press charges, if that's what you're worried about.'

'What?' he asked, looking bewildered. 'What do you mean?'

'I mean we both know that you took advantage of me, but I won't go to the police. You'd only end up in a young offender institution, where God only knows what would happen to you, and I don't want that on my conscience.'

'But I . . . I didn't . . . it was you who—'

'As far as I'm concerned, none of this ever happened. But you should count yourself lucky. Anyone else in my place would have had you arrested by now.'

He stared at me, shook his head slowly, then started crying again.

'But I need you to go,' I continued. 'And don't ever come back here again. If you do, I'll report you. You'll end up as a convicted sex offender. Your parents will disown you. Your entire life will be ruined. Is that what you want?'

'No,' he whispered.

'Good. Well, you've been warned.'

He pulled himself to his feet and made his way back into the living room, walking so unsteadily towards the front door that, if I hadn't known better, I would have assumed he was inebriated. When he reached it, he struggled with the lock and I had to open it for him. When my hand brushed his arm, he pushed me away. Then – Christ alive – the tears again.

'What the fuck is the matter with you?' I asked. 'I'm trying to help you here.'

'I didn't want it,' he said.

'Didn't want what?'

'That. What we did.'

'Then why did you do it?'

'You made me.'

'Did I drag you into my car?' I asked, raising my voice

now. 'Because I seem to remember you opening the door of your own accord. Did I force you up to my apartment? You came willingly enough. Did I pour Coke over your T-shirt so you'd have to take it off? I don't think so. I'm pretty sure that was you. Very subtle, by the way.'

'It exploded over—'

'Take responsibility for what you did, Rufus. You haven't even apologized.'

'I'm . . .' He looked around, his face falling, completely disoriented.

'Look, I'm a grown woman,' I said, trying to sound magnanimous. 'Believe me, I'm used to the violence of men. I don't know what's going on in your life, but maybe from now on you'll realize that you can't treat girls like this. Not everyone will be as willing to forgive as me.'

He nodded.

'I'm sorry,' he said.

'As you should be.'

He paused for a few moments, then looked at me, genuinely curious.

'You really didn't want that?' he asked tentatively.

'Rufus,' I said, in as measured a tone as I could muster, 'you raped me. You understand that, right? You are a rapist. That's something you're going to have to live with for the rest of your life.'

He seemed uncertain what to do next, so I decided the only way to get rid of him was to drive him home. We travelled down to the garage in silence, and when he placed his bag in the back seat, he sat there too, rather than joining me in the front. For the first time, I noticed that his school backpack had two badges sewn into it. One for the city's football team – the same team whose erstwhile players I had once sat in judgement upon – and one bearing a picture of the Muppets. I felt embarrassed for him. It was the sort of thing a child would have. We didn't speak as we drove, other than him giving me quiet directions, and when I finally pulled up outside his small, terraced house, he leapt out of the car like a jack-in-the-box, disappearing inside without so much as a goodbye.

I haven't given him a second thought since then, but now, when there's a knock on my door, for some reason his face pops into my mind, even though I know it can't be him. It must be Hugh Winley, I tell myself, coming up to try it on with me again. He'll be standing outside with a bottle of wine, saying he's just opened it but doesn't want to drink alone. I'll have to be firm with him. Tell him once and for all that I'm not interested. He has a certain malevolence to him, though, that is perhaps not uncommon in children's television presenters, and I assume he'll react badly to a definitive rejection.

However, when I open the door, it's not my neighbour standing there, and as it turns out, I rather wish it was.

It is, however, a fourteen-year-old boy. When I recognize his face, my heart sinks.

Those phone calls where no one spoke when I answered. And then the one where he did, on the very same evening that I picked Rufus up from his football game.

Is that Freya?

'Hi,' he says, the very definition of a shit-eating grin on his face. 'Remember me?'

'Graham,' I say, knowing full well that I'm getting his name wrong but not wanting him to think that I remember it. My heart is beating a little faster in my chest. I've never slept with a boy twice. I've never needed to. It's not as if I actually enjoy the experience, after all. I just want to destroy their chances of ever forming happy, healthy relationships in the future.

'George,' he says, correcting me. 'George Eliot. Like the writer, remember?' He walks brazenly past me, marching into the living room, followed by an overwhelming stink of cheap cologne. I stare at his back and offer a slight laugh before closing the door. If I could, I would pause the universe for a moment and think this through. Whatever made him repeatedly call me, and whatever has brought him here tonight, I need to play it very carefully.

'Did you miss me?' he asks, turning around.

'What are you doing here?' I ask, folding my arms across my chest. Although I'm wearing loungewear, my feet are bare, and I feel exposed. I can't just throw him out, because that would risk antagonizing him and children his age are extremely unpredictable. I need to figure out what he wants. And then deny him it.

'I wanted to see you again,' he said. 'That's OK, isn't it?'

'How did you find me?' I ask.

'Ah,' he says, throwing himself down on the sofa and pulling his phone from his pocket. 'That is a really good question, and I think you'll be impressed. I actually spent the last few weeks trying to remember where you lived, and I just couldn't do it. I mean, I literally walked the streets day after day trying to find this building. You brought me quite a distance from my home, didn't you? But then it finally occurred to me.' He holds his phone up and waves it at me. 'These things track your movements. All I had to do was go back to the night we fucked, and it would tell me where I was. It pinned it down to the exact location. I don't know why I didn't think of it before.'

I flinch when he says the word 'fucked', but I'm even more disturbed to learn that smartphones track our movements. Does that mean that every boy I've ever brought here has a record of where he's been? If this is true, then it's very concerning.

'You phoned me, didn't you?' I ask. 'Called my number over and over, then hung up when I answered.'

'To be fair, I spoke once. But, after that, I couldn't get through again.'

'I thought you were a cold caller,' I lie. 'So I blocked you.'

'Who talks on the phone anyway?' he asks. 'Old people. No offence.'

'How did you get my number?'

'After we fucked,' he says, and I recoil again at his casual use of the word, 'you went into the bathroom but left your phone on the bedside table. By the way, just so you know, IIII is literally the dumbest passcode ever. It's the first thing everyone tries. So I just called my own phone, then deleted the call from your log and stored you in my contacts.'

I sit down in the armchair opposite him. 'I see,' I reply, wondering what would happen if I took him out to the balcony and just pushed him over. We're twelve floors up, after all. Every bone in his body would break and his skull would smash into a dozen pieces. But there's always someone from the opposite building outside having a smoke and I wouldn't get away with it. 'Well, it's nice to see you again, Graham.'

'George.'

'Sorry, George. Yes. But why are you here?'

'Isn't it obvious?'

'Not to me.'

He shrugs his shoulders.

'I'm horny.'

I notice that my left hand is tapping nervously on the armrest and I force myself to remain still. I don't want him to feel that he has any hold over me.

'That's a really inappropriate thing to say,' I say, giving him my best Miss Jean Brodie.

'I mean, it would be, yeah,' he says, scratching his chin, 'if we hadn't already done it. But since we have, it doesn't seem so bad.'

'That was a mistake,' I say. 'And I decided not to take it any further.'

'Take what any further?' he asks, frowning.

'What you did to me,' I say.

'I don't get it.'

'Well, you took advantage of me,' I tell him.

He laughs, which makes me want to take a baseball bat to his head.

'*I* took advantage of *you*?' he asks. 'Look, I'm not gonna lie. I loved every moment of it. But it's you who did that to me, not the other way round. You're the adult. I'm the child. You picked me up outside the hospital, told me where to meet you later, collected me, brought me here. I was just visiting a mate. I wasn't, like, on the pull. Anyway, fuck that, you need to be honest with yourself, Freya. I can call you Freya, right? It was amazing, wasn't it? I literally haven't stopped thinking about it ever since. I bet you haven't either. It's why I've been trying to find you.'

'Well,' I say, realizing that I need to change tack as it's obvious that he won't be easily threatened. 'I'm glad you enjoyed yourself, but it was a one-off.'

'No, it wasn't,' he says, brushing this away and looking around the room as if he's considering moving in.

'It was.'

'Nope.'

I stare at him, wondering what my next move should be. I've never been put in this position before and am uncertain how to handle it.

'You need to leave,' I say.

'No problem.'

'Thank you.'

'After we do it.'

I feel a sense of panic overwhelming me. The earth is falling on my coffin, I'm searching for my breathing tube and pushing against the roof, begging Arthur and Pascoe to release me. But they're not there. They've gone home. I'm buried alive.

'That's not going to happen,' I say forcefully.

'It sure is.'

'It's not.'

'Why not?'

'Because you're just a kid.'

He throws his head back and laughs, as if this is the greatest joke in the world. 'Seriously?' he asks. 'I mean, come on.'

'You need to leave,' I repeat. 'What happened then, that night, it was a mistake.'

'If it was, then it's one that I want to repeat. Over and over and over and—'

'Have you told anyone about this?' I ask.

'Just my mate,' he says. 'My best mate. Harry. You remember Harry.'

I stare at him, wondering whether he's gone completely mad.

'How would I know your friend Harry?' I ask.

'He's the one in your hospital,' he tells me. 'Who needs the kidney transplant.'

'Oh yes,' I say, vaguely remembering our conversation on the day we met.

'You can relax, he didn't believe me. And I didn't tell him who it was either. I just said an older woman had popped my cherry.'

'Has no one ever told you that you're not supposed to kiss and tell?' I ask.

'I didn't kiss and tell,' he says, sitting forward and opening his arms wide. 'I fucked and told. Big difference. Anyway, like I said, he didn't believe me. Thinks I made it all up. Not that it matters. I know it happened, and you know it happened, and that's enough. But maybe tonight, when we're doing it, we can take a photo? So I can show him? I'll keep your face out of it, I promise. Just, like, the rest of you. Your tits and stuff. And my face in it so he knows I'm not lying.'

'George,' I say, trying to remain calm. 'I'm not going to say this again. You need to leave.'

'Or what?'

'Or I'll call the police.'

He sits back now and smiles. Uses his left hand to mimic a phone being held to his ear.

'Good evening, Constable,' he says. 'I'm a thirty-something woman who picked up an underage boy a few weeks ago and took him back to my apartment and had sex with him. I know that's against the law, but let's just forget that for now because he's in my apartment and refuses to leave. Can you send someone over to throw him out?'

Maybe there'll be no one outside smoking. Maybe my timing will be perfect and I can simply toss him over the side.

'I'm not going to have sex with you,' I insist.

'Sure you are,' he replies.

'And what,' I ask, 'makes you so sure of that?'

To my annoyance, he makes himself at home by using the toe of his right foot to kick off his left trainer, then his left to kick off the right, revealing once-white socks that look like they've been through the washer about a thousand times.

'Because,' he tells me, 'if you don't, I'll tell.'

9

IT'S LATE AFTERNOON AND I'm preparing for a surgery taking place in two days' time. A man named Richard Conway, separated from his wife of four years, waited outside their former marital home until she returned from work, then approached her as she put her key in the door. When she turned, he sprayed her with lighter fluid before tossing a lit match in her direction, resulting in third-degree burns to her right arm, neck, breasts, and the lower half of her face. I plan on doing a skin graft that should hopefully repair some of the damage he caused, although she will never, of course, look as she once did.

I've dealt with crimes like this more often than I can count. I've seen women whose faces have been destroyed by the men who stood next to them at an altar promising to spend their lives together. Women who know they'll never willingly look in a mirror again. Women who've gone through dozens of operations just to stop people staring at them on the street, on a bus, or in a supermarket. Wasn't it Margaret Atwood who said that men are afraid that women will laugh at them, but women are afraid that men will kill them? In Conway's case, he didn't want his wife dead; he just wanted to make sure that no other man would ever want her again.

I've invited Aaron to assist at the operation. And when I say assist, I mean observe. He's still too green to hold a scalpel, but it will be good for him to witness what takes place in theatre. Louise appears pleased, if a little surprised, when I mention this to her.

'You're warming to him, then?' she asks.

'Well, I wouldn't go that far,' I say. 'But I'm making an effort, like you suggested. Actually, I invited him for a drink.'

'You didn't!'

'I did. I thought it might help if I got to know him a little better.'

'And?'

'Well, it wasn't the best evening of my life, but it wasn't the worst either. He's polite, interested, curious. His girlfriend's training to be a pilot, did you know that?'

'How would I?'

'I thought the pair of you talked.'

'We do,' she says. 'But he plays his cards close to his chest, that one. Still, I'm not surprised he's got a girlfriend. He's a bit of a looker, don't you think?'

'Not my type.'

'Too young?'

I glance at my watch and think about the final episode of a drama series that I've been saving to watch tonight. I think about my Ocado order. I think about an award-winning novel I've been reading but that I can't get to grips with. I think about anything but her question.

'With retirement looming,' she continues when I fail to answer, 'I wonder should I start looking for a younger man.'

'You don't think Liam would mind?' I ask, referring to her husband, with whom she has a very loving relationship.

'Sure he would, but he doesn't have to know, does he? From what I read, all the twenty-something boys are mooning over older women these days. It's that pop star, what's-his-name. The lad from the boy band. Always going after them.'

There's an awkward moment as she realizes that I'm not engaging with her banter in the way that I usually would.

'So, was there a spark?' she asks eventually.

'I'm sorry?'

'A spark,' she repeats. 'Between you and Aaron. On your date.'

'It wasn't a date,' I say, rolling my eyes.

'You asked him out.'

'No, he asked me.'

'Did you not just say, "Actually, I invited him for a drink"?'

I'm thrown for a moment. She's right. I did say that.

'I meant that I agreed to go for one, that's all. He wanted to discuss his career in a less, you know, formal environment than the hospital.'

'And when did all this take place?'

'A couple of weekends ago.'

I'm fond of Louise, but the expression on her face, that

self-satisfied smile, is annoying, and I regret bringing the subject up at all.

'Trust me,' I tell her, 'I have absolutely no ambitions in that direction.'

'If you say so.'

'He's practically a child,' I insist. 'What do you take me for?'

Perhaps my tone is more aggressive than I intended because she looks a little put out.

'All right,' she says. 'I was only teasing.'

'Well, don't,' I say.

Perhaps it will be better, after all, when she's no longer here. There should be clear lines drawn between doctors and nurses, and we've grown too familiar with each other.

Aaron is with me now, studying my surgical plan, when my pager goes off and I'm summoned downstairs to A&E. I move quickly and he follows like an obedient puppy, although he waits for the elevator while I take the stairs, which means he has to run to catch up with me when Holly, one of the more experienced nurses down here, sees me approaching and offers a quick nod of acknowledgement before handing me a clipboard.

'House fire,' she says. 'Thirty-two-year-old female, nine-year-old male, seven-year-old female, two-year-old infant.'

I scan the notes prepared by the ambulance crews, flicking through pages, knowing exactly what I'm looking for and taking in every relevant piece of information. When I push open the door to the area where they're being treated, a team of nurses and junior doctors is already attending to them and I'm hit with the familiar smell of charred flesh along with the equally recognizable sound of suffering, a low keening emerging from beneath gauze-covered bodies as cannulas are inserted into veins and morphine is injected to deliver some relief from the pain. I quickly establish that the mother is unlikely to survive while the two-year-old has already been covered with a sheet and I instruct a porter to remove him to the morgue. The older children are still alive but only the girl looks perceptibly human. From behind me, a sound of deep distress arises from Aaron.

'If you're going to throw up, take it outside,' I say, and he turns and runs.

Over the next hour, I prescribe medication, order tests, and do all that I can to alleviate the pain of the three remaining victims. The nine-year-old boy's organs are beginning to shut down and all I can do is make his transition from this world to the next as painless as possible. Most of my attention needs to be turned towards his younger sister, who's suffered the least amount of trauma but whose future is irrevocably changed. Earlier today, she would have been a perfectly normal-looking child with her entire life before her. She would have gone on to meet a boy or girl someday and fallen in love. She would have broken hearts and had her heart broken. She might have taken trips to the Grand Canyon, the Great Barrier Reef, Victoria Falls. She might have become an award-winning actress, the managing director of a tech firm or an employee in an organic-food shop. But none of those things are likely to happen now. She's too young for her skin to heal. Her life will be defined by pain and, most likely, an endless series of operations.

When Aaron returns, he's steeled himself for the wretchedness contained within this room and walks towards the boy, taking his hand in his and holding it gently. I can't hear what he's saying but he's speaking to the child in a low, calming voice and the boy is moving his charred fingers a little, as if he's trying to squeeze my intern's hand.

Seven minutes later, he dies.

Thirteen minutes after that, his mother passes away too.

The girl is made as comfortable as possible before being moved upstairs to the specialist burns unit, where she will become my priority over the next twenty-four to forty-eight hours. When there's a moment to breathe, I make my way outside the hospital and close my eyes, throwing my head back in a desperate need to inhale some fresh air, even though I contradict this by lighting a cigarette. Three hours have passed since we were summoned downstairs, but it feels like only a fraction of that time. Aaron joins me but remains silent as he leans up against the wall.

'Are you all right?' I ask, offering him a smoke too, but he declines.

'Yes,' he says. 'Sorry about earlier.'

'Don't be,' I tell him. 'Situations like that take some getting used to.'

I hesitate, then pay him a rare compliment.

'When you came back in, Aaron, you did a good job. I saw you comforting the boy. We might not have been able to save him, but you showed great empathy.'

He offers a half-smile. 'I thought you said that we should keep emotion out of the job?'

'I did,' I admit. 'But sometimes that's impossible. We're only human, after all.'

'Are we?' he asks.

'Well, aren't we?'

He shrugs. 'I don't know, sometimes. Someone did that to them.'

'Of course someone did.'

'A man.'

'Probably.'

'Men like that—'

'Are less rare than you might think.'

'You say that like we're the only monsters.'

'You know a lot of female serial killers, do you? Female rapists? Women murdering their husbands?'

'Not many, no. But I don't think one sex is more inherently evil than the other.'

I shake my head. It feels pointless arguing with him. His generation always believe they're right about everything. Their sense of moral superiority is what makes them so unbearable.

'I mean it, Freya,' he says, surprising me in his use of my first name. 'Think of that little boy we treated a couple of months back. Vidar. It was his mother who was abusing him and her husband.'

'True,' I admit.

'And I've seen some other things while I've been here.'

'I'm not saying women are perfect,' I say. 'Or that we're always the victims. I'm simply saying that, more often than not, men are the perpetrators of violence against us, not the other way round.'

'Everyone I know, all my friends, we have mothers, sisters, girlfriends, ex-girlfriends, we had female teachers, we have female bosses, we've been surrounded by women, just like you've been surrounded by men, and some of us have scars too. Not scars like they have, of course,' he adds, pointing back towards the hospital, where our most recent patients lie. 'Not the sort you can see. But they exist all the same.'

He's speaking quietly but passionately, displaying his empathy once again, and I realize how, more than any other intern who's ever studied under me, he'll develop into a brilliant doctor. Surprisingly, I feel an almost maternal pride in him.

'You're a good man, Aaron,' I say, the words out of my mouth before I even knew I was going to utter them.

He turns to me, and I expect a smile of gratitude, but instead he's frowning. He looks like he's about to say something unexpectedly aggressive, but before he can, a man approaches and introduces himself as the detective assigned to the case.

'What happened?' I ask. 'Do you know yet?'

'There's history,' he tells me.

'What kind of history?'

'The husband,' he says, confirming what both Aaron and I had already suspected. 'The wife was in a shelter. He couldn't track her down. The council found temporary accommodation for her, he found out where, came over and set the place alight.'

'His own children?' asks Aaron, looking aghast. 'He'd do that to his own children?'

'She pushed him too far, I guess,' the detective says. 'There was a custody hearing due to take place on—'

'She pushed him too far?' Aaron asks, raising his voice, the first time since he arrived on my rotation that I've seen him express anger. 'I'm sorry, but . . . what the fuck?'

'No, I didn't mean—'

'What, there's a point she can push him to, and after that he can't be held responsible for his actions?'

The policeman stares at Aaron for a few moments before turning to me.

'You might want to ask this young man to control his emotions,' he says. 'Those kinds of comments do nothing to help the situation.'

'Fuck you,' I tell him, and a staring competition begins between us. He's overweight and trying for movie-star stubble but only looks like he was too lazy to shave. I glance at his left hand and see the tell-tale whiteness on the flabby fourth finger of his left hand where a wedding ring used to be. There's no point arguing with men like him. Eventually, when the case is built, he'll be in touch, and I'll find myself in a courtroom testifying to what took place. A prosecution barrister will tell the jury why the husband should spend years in jail for his crime, while a defence barrister will offer reasons why the jury should let him get away with it. And twelve people will decide. As I did a few years ago. They might get it right or, like me, they might get it badly wrong.

'All I meant was—' he begins, but I shake my head, cutting him off before he can say anything else.

'Dr Umber is right,' I tell him. 'You can't say things like that. Three people are dead, two of them children. A fourth is in a critical condition. And instinctively, whether you intended to or not, you blamed the victim. You blamed the woman.'

'It was a turn of phrase, that's all.'

There's no point continuing to argue the toss. He'll fight his corner to the death, men like him always do, especially when arguing with women, so I simply turn away and make my way back inside and along the corridor towards the nurses' station. Holly is still on shift and asks me how things went. I shake my head, and she's experienced enough to understand what this means without any words needing to be exchanged. Around us, gurneys pass by while outside, in the waiting room, people sit with broken arms, sprained ankles, knife wounds, all the injuries that human beings suffer on a daily basis because our skin is only so thick and our bones only so resilient and from the moment we arrive on the planet the universe is against us, conspiring to drown us, set us on fire, bury us in the earth, our spirits floating off into the atmosphere.

I'm about to return to the staircase and the comfort of my office when a fresh gurney is pushed through the doors, followed by two paramedics and a woman in her late thirties. I glance towards the patient. Around his neck I see dark purple bruises that tell me he's tried to hang himself. Emergency doctors rush towards him while I take a step back; it's not my department and I know better than to get in their way. They check his blood pressure, his heartbeat, his eyes. They place a mask over his mouth and feed him oxygen. The woman accompanying him – his mother, I assume – is distraught, telling us that she heard a loud noise from his bedroom, which turned out to be the sound of a chair being overturned. She ran upstairs, discovered him, but was too weak to cut him down. She held his legs, trying to keep him elevated for as long as she could, while he kicked and struggled against the tension of the noose he'd created for himself with his school tie. Finally, she let his legs go, reached for some scissors from his desk, and jumped on his bed to cut away at the fabric, and he fell to the ground, unconscious.

'They weren't even sharp, the scissors,' she tells us, looking around at each of us in turn, her eyes desperate with fear. 'Just a kid's scissors, you know? Blunt ones. For his arts and crafts. He loves his arts and crafts. He always has, since he was a child. So they're blunt. You know. For children. So they don't hurt themselves. I couldn't get them to tear away at the fabric.'

I've been a doctor for a long time, and I can usually tell, simply by looking at a patient, what their chances are. This boy is still breathing, but there's little hope. He'll be placed on a life-support machine almost immediately and within a few hours, or a day at most, his mother will be told there's nothing more that can be done for him, that brain activity is non-existent, and then she will have to make the decision to turn the machine off. In the moment of her most extreme grief, she'll be asked whether she'll allow his organs to be donated.

'What's his name?' asks one of the A&E doctors, and although the boy's mother is the one to answer, I hear the words emerge from my lips at the same time, so quietly that the chances of anyone overhearing me are almost impossible.

'Rufus,' I whisper. 'His name is Rufus.'

10

L YING IN MY MAKESHIFT coffin, I slowly began to understand that there is only one thing crueller or more
virulent than a fourteen-year-old boy: two of them.

At first, I had been terrified, convinced that I would
quickly run out of oxygen and die beneath the earth. The
breathing tube the twins had fed through the ground
worked well enough, but even so, every breath I sucked
desperately into my lungs felt as if it might be my last.
The darkness contributed to my panic. I heard sounds, or
imagined I did. Sometimes I found myself laughing
hysterically, then breaking down in tears. As the hours
passed, I started to imagine that the outside world was a
fantasy and that only here, inside my tomb, was reality.
Occasionally, I pinched myself, wondering whether I'd
succumbed to some horrible nightmare. I dozed, then
woke with a shock, my hands pressing impotently against
the ceiling.

I found ways to pass the time. I sang my favourite
songs over and over. At school, I'd memorized the names
of all the English kings and queens, from William the
Conqueror to Elizabeth II, and I recited them backwards.
I thought of every job that began with the letter 'M' and

every country that started with the letter 'A'. I came up with the most disgusting ways to destroy the lives of fourteen-year-old boys. I decided upon the meal I would have eaten, had I known this would be my last night on earth. I composed letters in my head, one to Hannah and one to Beth, telling them what terrible parents, or surrogate parents, they had been. I counted my fingers and toes and became convinced that I had nine of the former and eleven of the latter. I tried to remember as many of Black Beauty's owners as I could. I closed my eyes and dreamed of wide-open spaces. I cried. I laughed. I made popping noises with my mouth. I think, at one point, I slept.

When I finally heard the sound of the soil being cleared from above me, I panicked again, uncertain what fresh torture might be in store for me, and when the lid was lifted at last and the morning sun shone down on my face I was momentarily blinded. As my eyes adjusted, however, I recognized the faces of the boys kneeling in the soil, looking down at me with anxious expressions. The birthmark on Arthur's neck seemed more pronounced than ever and they appeared surprised, even frightened, when I didn't immediately leap from my improvised grave.

'Freya,' said Pascoe, reaching a hand down, his voice filled with fear. 'Freya, are you all right?'

I stared at his hand, uncertain whether to take it.

'Come on, Freya,' said Arthur. 'It was a joke, that's all. A game. Don't be mad at us.'

So, this was the second game we had played. Which

was worse? I wondered. One that involved my being repeatedly raped in a cave or one that saw me being buried alive? And if there was to be a third, what form might that take? Perhaps they would tie me to a wall and throw axes at me. Or take me to the top of the cliffs and hang me over by my ankles.

Slowly, I felt the warmth return to my body and I sat up cautiously, my back aching from the long hours I had spent lying in the same position. Pulling myself to my feet, I felt my knees tremble as I exhumed myself. To my right, I noticed a long steel pole discarded by the builders in the dirt and considered picking it up and bashing their brains in with it. Then I thought, no, I'll kill just one of them. That would hurt more. I was familiar enough with their ways to know that neither could possibly survive without the other.

'We didn't mean to leave you there for so long,' said Arthur, doing his best to sound repentant. 'It was only meant to be for an hour or two. But we fell asleep. Father didn't come home – we usually wake when he does – so we couldn't come back. We don't know where he is.'

He looked at me as if he expected me to offer an explanation for Kitto's absence, but it was the furthest thing from my mind.

'You buried me,' I whispered, my voice grainy. I was dehydrated, badly in need of water. 'You left me to die.'

'It was a game,' he repeated, and I turned to Pascoe, who appeared far less contrite than his twin. If anything, he looked mildly irritated, as if he considered it something of a bore that I wasn't willing to laugh along at their actions. Arthur moved forward and, worried that he was going to put me back where he'd found me, I pushed him away. He stumbled, almost falling into the pit himself. I ran from them both, my unsteady legs gathering strength as I raced towards the beach. When I reached the shoreline, I ran into the water, desperate for the sea to cleanse me.

I remained there a long time, swimming much further out than I'd intended. I could swim to France if I wanted, I told myself. I could drown. I could escape them all.

On the shoreline I saw the twins waving for me to return. Their heads were pressed together, locked in conversation. I guessed that they were frightened, just as I had been frightened. Fearful of what I might do, who I might tell. There were so many ways that I could cause trouble for them, after all. The cave; the grave; these waves. Their telling me that their father had murdered their mother. I had rarely thought of this since they'd first mentioned it, but it came back to me now as I floated there, wondering whether it might, in fact, be true. If the boys were psychopaths, then it stood to reason that Kitto might be one too.

Eventually, I returned to the beach, stepping on to the sand and walking past them, ignoring their attempts to talk to me. As I made my way back in the direction of the cottage, it pleased me to think that they would spend the hours and days ahead worrying about what might happen next.

Back home, I found Beth lying on the sofa, smoking a cigarette and watching one of those Saturday-morning television shows aimed at teenagers. Scattered on the carpet were empty beer cans, and she waved in their direction, not taking her eyes off the screen, utterly oblivious to my soaking clothes, and instructed me to clear them up. She was barefoot, wearing a tracksuit, and hadn't showered yet, her make-up from the previous night streaked across her face.

'You were up and about early,' she muttered, and I knew then that she hadn't even been aware of my absence the night before. From the bathroom, I heard the sound of the toilet flushing and the taps turning on, and, glancing down the corridor, I expected to see Eli emerge through the door, his usual smile on his face when he saw me. But when the door to the living room opened, it wasn't Eli who stepped into the room, it was Kitto Teague. I stared at him, unable to comprehend his presence here. He paused for a moment and frowned, as if he wasn't entirely sure who I was.

'Where's Eli?' I asked, turning to Beth, and she shrugged her shoulders, took a long drag from her cigarette, then laughed at something one of the television presenters said, before answering.

'Eli's history,' she said. 'He's gone. And good riddance too.'

'Gone where?'

'To the unemployment office, I expect,' said Kitto, sitting down on one of the kitchen chairs and reaching for his shoes. 'Three weeks behind schedule,' he added, his voice so refined that it seemed almost comical, as if he was putting it on. A cartoon Englishman in an American film. 'That's what I get for hiring a yokel rather than bringing a professional down from London. I should have got rid of him long ago.'

'Ditto,' said Beth.

He walked over to the sofa and retrieved his coat, leaning over and whispering something in Beth's ear. She muted the television for a moment before looking up at him.

'I don't see why not,' she replied to whatever it was he'd said. 'Only, just so you know, I'm not here for a bunk-up any time you've got ants in your pants. Take me somewhere nice next time, all right? Somewhere fancy though, not just down the pub for cod and chips and mushy peas. I can get that any time.'

'Let's wait and see,' he replied quietly. He made his way towards me, narrowing his eyes as he looked me up and down. For a moment, I thought he might prise my jaws apart and check my teeth.

'You're friends with my sons, aren't you?' he asked, and I nodded. It seemed pointless to try to explain the complicated nature of our relationship, which even I did not fully understand. 'Do you have a favourite?'

'A favourite?' I asked, frowning.

'Yes, among the two of them,' he said. 'Is there one of them that you like more than the other?'

I stared at him. It had never occurred to me to separate them in any way. They seemed like a composite being to me. They had always been the twins. Arthur and Pascoe.

'Or perhaps one that you dislike less?' he continued. 'Personally, I've always preferred Pascoe. Arthur can be querulous. And I find that birthmark of his unsightly. Their mother was a twin too, as was her father. It's not a Teague trait. I find it faintly ridiculous, if I'm honest. Their devotion to each other embarrasses me too. I'd prefer they fought, as boys do, not carried on as if they've got some unholy crush on each other. I'd rather hoped you might come between them, in fact. That they'd fight over you. Anyway . . .'

He drifted off for a moment and glanced around the room with a sigh, as if he was considering whether or not he should put the rent up or simply burn the place down. 'Don't tell either of them I said that, will you?' He reached down and took my chin in his hands. 'No one likes a tattle-tale.' Then he leaned over and kissed me gently on the lips, lingering there for a moment while Beth watched and took a long, slow drag on her cigarette as she observed us.

'It doesn't really have to be somewhere fancy, Mr Teague,' she called out as he left. 'I was only joking. The local is as good as anywhere.'

He didn't reply, merely raised a hand in the air without looking back. Beth, on the other hand, wore a hopeful expression on her face. I found it surprising that she would address him in such a formal way. If they had slept together, as I assumed they had, then surely she could at least call him by his first name.

'I think I might be on to something there, sweetheart,' she said, rubbing the thumb and index finger of her right hand together in the universal sign for money. Her cigarette fell as she did so, dropping on to the floor, but she didn't seem to notice as it connected with a newspaper, igniting a small but determined flame. I watched as the pages rose in anger, knowing I should say something but choosing to remain silent. It took another thirty seconds before she realized that the heat around her ankles was the beginnings of a fire and she quickly stamped it out.

I remained in my room for the rest of the day, stretched out on my bed. Although I was exhausted, whenever I closed my eyes I imagined myself back in my coffin with the sound of the earth falling on the lid and the cramped walls closing in on me. I was only twelve years old that summer, but I was mature enough to know that I would think about what had taken place during those months for the rest of my life.

Still, I reassured myself that all was not lost. After all, there was still a week left before I was due to return to Norfolk. There was still time to set things right.

II

I T's the seventh time that George has shown up at my apartment, but at least he no longer arrives unannounced. Instead, he texts when he wants sex, and I've learned that I can only get away with saying no twice in a row before he becomes threatening, leaving me with no choice but to invite him over. I take no pleasure in our encounters and have grown to despise both his smug little face and the tawdry remarks he makes, thinking they might put me in the mood. I have no idea how much porn the boy watches – quite a lot, I imagine, if his words and actions are anything to go by – but he clearly hasn't the first clue how women in the real world behave or what we want from our sexual encounters.

We don't, for example, want our hair pulled. Nor do we want to be choked. It's not a turn-on to be called by the names that men have historically called women in their attempts to demean them. We would prefer that our partners ejaculated into condoms rather than on to our faces. Rape fantasies are not an actual thing, although rapes themselves are. We're not interested in filming our encounters and subsequently uploading them to the internet, nor do we particularly enjoy watching the erotic encounters of others. Thanks to unfettered access to Wi-Fi since before he even reached puberty, however, these are clearly the things that George believes are the fastest way to a girl's heart. And to think: people used to say it with flowers.

Today, he turns fifteen, which is the final nail in the coffin in terms of any interest I might ever have displayed in him, and to my dismay he insists on spending his birthday with me, making it clear in advance that he expects me to do something special to mark the occasion. I thought this meant a cake and a present, but no, he sent me a link for a High Neck Halter Lace Bodysuit from Victoria's Secret and said that he wanted me to wear it on what he called his 'special night'. I did as instructed. For the time being, at least, I have no choice.

He's confided in me a few times about his home life, apparently believing that I care about his regular arguments with his father and his non-existent relationship with his mother, who left when he was four years old and moved to Jersey, starting a new family there that didn't involve him. He visits every summer for a month, just as I did with Beth when I was a child, but he tells me that she barely tolerates his presence, while his stepfather and step-siblings actively resent him.

'Maybe we could go together sometime?' he asks, and I glance across the room from where I'm preparing his birthday dinner, his favourite and a gourmand's delight: chicken nuggets, chips and beans.

'Go where?' I ask.

'To Jersey,' he says. 'To my mum's.'

I stare at him in disbelief.

'Why on earth would we do that?'

'Because I'd like you to meet her. You're my girlfriend, after all, and she's my mum. You'll need to get to know each other sooner or later.'

It takes all my self-control not to burst out laughing.

'George,' I say, keeping my tone steady as I can't risk provoking him. 'I'm not your girlfriend.'

'Of course you are,' he replies, looking genuinely surprised, even wounded. 'We're sleeping together, aren't we?'

'That's just a physical act,' I tell him. 'And a private one. But we're not actually dating. We've never even been outside this flat together.'

'I was thinking about that too,' he says, coming over and taking my right hand in his sweaty little fist. The urge to pull it away and wipe it on my trousers is over-whelming. 'Don't you think we should do something other than just, you know, have sex?'

'I'd be very happy not to have sex with you, George.'

He frowns. Perhaps I'm being too subtle for him.

'Like, we could go to a film together some night. The new Transformers movie comes out next week.'

'The what?' I ask.

'You're kidding, right?'

I shrug.

'Oh my God,' he shouts, growing animated now. 'It's a series of movies about these machines that—'

'How many are there?' I ask.

'Machines?'

'No, movies.'

'I don't know. A bunch. We could watch all the old ones here across a few nights – I could stay over – and then go to the IMAX to see the new one. What do you think?'

I think that I'd rather dig a hole to the centre of the earth with my tongue.

'Sure,' I say. 'Sounds like a plan.'

'Great. Sorted.'

He then starts talking about the Marvel Cinematic Universe, which has apparently spawned dozens of films, and says that we can start on them once our triumphant journey through the world of Transformers has come to an end.

'I can't believe you haven't seen any of them,' he says, looking genuinely baffled. 'Like, I thought people your age were really into cinema?'

'I like Almodóvar,' I tell him. 'And Woody Allen. And Jane Campion.'

He stares at me in complete bewilderment, as if I've just started speaking Latin. I shake my head. There's no point explaining. To my ennui, he begins a long and erudite analysis of the virtues of Ironman, Thor and Captain America, and it takes all my willpower to stop myself from telling him that I would rather have my eyeballs prised out with nail scissors than subject myself to any of these celluloid atrocities.

'And if we plan on going to my mum's at some point,' he continues, bringing the conversation back to where it started, but sounding a little more cautious now, 'then, before that, maybe I could introduce you to some of my friends.'

I open the fridge door to hide my face from him as I let out a silent scream. 'George,' I say. 'You haven't told anyone about us, have you?'

'No,' he says. 'I swear I haven't. You told me not to.'

'You know how much trouble I could get into if any of this got out, right?'

'I do,' he says, smiling now, knowing the power he has over me. 'You could go to jail.'

He's too young to be a good liar and I'm reasonably confident that he's telling the truth, but at the same time, I'm also conscious that a teenage boy having regular sex with a thirty-six-year-old woman will, at some point, brag about it to his friends. He'd probably enjoy the kudos just as much as the sex itself, if not more, and it would only take a single party, two or three beers, or a joint, before he let it slip, and then word would spread from boy to boy before it found its way back to me in the form of two members of His Majesty's constabulary knocking on my front door, wanting a word.

But my confidence does not equate to certainty, which is why I brought some sleeping tablets back from the hospital this evening, crushed them, and dropped them into the bottle of beer that he always drinks when he arrives. I'm standing in the doorway of my bedroom now, watching him while he sleeps. He looks ridiculously young and innocent, his mouth a little open, his fringe falling in his eyes. No one looking at him would suspect that he's a blackmailer. They'd think he was a perfectly nice kid.

I pick up his jeans from the bedroom floor and take his
phone from his back pocket, switching it to mute, and
hold it in front of his face to unlock the home screen.
When it opens, I take it into the living room and begin a
forensic examination of its contents.

He has the same phone as me – albeit a much earlier
incarnation – which makes things simple as I'm familiar
with the operating system, but while I keep a very ordered
home screen, collecting all my apps in neatly organized
folders, his is utter chaos, a Jackson Pollock painting
splashed across dozens of pages in no conceivable order.
I've no idea what most of them do, but I start with the
basic Messages app, which is empty. I suppose that's too
old school for him. I try WhatsApp next, and only three
conversations are saved, a back-and-forth with his father,
another with someone called Steven, who, when I scroll
through them, seems to be his uncle. Neither contains
anything incriminating. His third communicant is someone called GF, which turns out to be me, and is a complete
log of every message we've shared, from my initial message on the day we first met outside the hospital to the
one he sent me earlier tonight telling me what time he'd
be arriving. I'm pleased that he hasn't entered me on his
contacts list by name, and it doesn't take me long to
figure out what *GF* means.

Girlfriend.

His social media doesn't include Facebook or Twitter –
even his parents have probably given up on them – but he
has Instagram, although he hasn't posted many pictures and
doesn't seem to reply to any of the messages he receives,

which tend to be a series of indecipherable emojis rather than actual words. I've heard of Snapchat but have never used it, and the fact that it's the first app on his home screen and has a bubble saying he has fifty-four unopened messages makes me realize that this is where most of his communications take place. I open it and try to understand how it works. The people he communicates with on there seem to have normal names, and within the messages themselves, things aren't much more literate. Thankfully, when I eventually translate them into English, none of the gibberish seems to refer to me.

Until I open one directed to *HarryCull2010*.

George has already admitted to me that he's told his friend Harry that he's sleeping with someone, but swore that he hasn't said who it is. To reassure myself of this, in recent weeks I've used the hospital's internal computer system to keep a close eye on the boy's progress. He's an outpatient now and is doing better than he was a few months ago, but he's still awaiting a second kidney transplant. Shortly after George started blackmailing me, I went down to his room one afternoon wearing my doctor's coat so he'd assume I had a reason to be there, and found him engrossed in an Agatha Christie novel. In other circumstances, I might have talked to him about how obsessed I'd been by her books when I was his age, but instead, I made small talk with him as I scanned his chart and asked how he found his dialysis.

'It's OK,' he said. 'I'm getting used to it.'

'You're very brave,' I told him. 'Do you have many visitors? When you stay in, I mean.'

'My mum and dad and my sisters,' he told me. 'And some friends.'

'They must be worried about you.'

'I guess,' he said. 'Most of them seem frightened.'

'Why?'

'Because I might die.' His tone was remarkably calm, and I rather admired his stoicism. 'They don't know how to deal with what I'm going through.'

I sat down next to him and placed a hand on the outline of his knee beneath the blanket. He stared at it for a moment, but I left it there, even when he tried to move away. 'Life and death aren't things a boy your age should have to worry about.'

'I don't have much choice,' he said. 'My best mate though, he's been really good.'

'Oh yes?' I asked. This was what I had come here for. 'What's his name?'

'George. George Eliot.'

'Like the writer.'

'Like the writer,' he agreed, smiling.

'And how long have you known each other?' I asked.

'Me and George? For ever. We live three doors apart and our mums are besties. We basically grew up together.'

'So he's like a brother?'

'I guess,' he said.

'He cares about you?'

He looked away then, perhaps embarrassed by the question. I shouldn't have expected a child his age to be able to cope with such an emotional remark, and when one of the nurses appeared to check on him, I said good-bye and returned upstairs.

And here is his name now on George's Snapchat.

HarryCull2010

The messages go back a long way – George must save them all – and most of them are utter nonsense, barely comprehensible to someone my age, but then I come across an exchange that frightens me:

made her cum twyce 2nite, writes George.
u gotta let me know who she is
cant shed kill me
she hot?
fuk yeh
pix or it dint hapn

And then, to my horror, there is a picture. Of me. Not, thankfully, of my face, but of my body. He'd asked for one before, of course, but I'd refused him. I must have fallen asleep after some encounter, however, and he took a photo of my breasts with his own face directed to the camera, offering a wide smile and the thumbs-up sign.

u lucky cunt
hahaha
like wtf
i no
howd u even
hoes be hoes
ledge

It goes back and forth with more drivel, but as obnoxious as the conversation becomes, I'm at least relieved that he never names me and there are no pictures that could identify me.

Still, it's only a matter of time.

Eventually, a sound from the bedroom makes me hide the phone down the side of my sofa and George wanders naked into the living room, looking a little disoriented after the effects of the pills I gave him.

'Do you have some water, bae?' he asks, making me cringe inside.

'Fridge,' I say.

When he makes his way towards it, I go into the bedroom and return his phone to the pocket of his jeans, glancing towards the bedsheets, which are in total disarray after our fifteen minutes of passion.

A moment later, he's behind me, his arms wrapped around my waist, and I know that he's about sixty seconds away from insisting that we have sex again. I turn around and smile.

'You're insatiable,' I say.

'You love it, you filthy bitch,' he tells me, pushing me down on to the bed, and I do exactly what he wants, offering no complaint, because I would prefer to comply with his wishes than find myself spending the next ten years in jail.

But really. This can't go on for ever. I refuse to be a victim any longer. It's time to act.

12

THE BAR IS QUITE busy but, thankfully, Louise has reserved a private area for her retirement party. I haven't socialized with people from the hospital in years, and if this gathering was being held for anyone else, the chances of me being here at all would be minimal. But Louise is the closest thing I've ever had to a friend at work, and it would be rude not to put in an appearance.

A curious thing happened on my way here. While making my way towards the venue, I saw Hugh Winley on the other side of the street, my ardent admirer from my apartment building, sitting in the open window of a separate bar with a young man of around his own age. I wouldn't have normally given it a second thought, but as I glanced in their direction, they leaned into each other and kissed. I watched for a moment, and when they separated, Hugh reached forward and placed his hand gently on his companion's cheek with an expression of total adoration on his face. Assuming he's gay, or at least bisexual, why on earth is he spending so much of his time trying to convince me to go on a date with him? I really don't understand young people any more. I don't know whether I admire their sexual fluidity or find it utterly narcissistic.

Glancing around now, I recognize some of my fellow doctors and surgeons, along with nurses and administration staff, and for a moment feel a twinge of envy that Louise inspires so much affection among our colleagues. If I was to resign tomorrow, I can't imagine anyone showing up to wish me well. One day, of course, I will walk out of the hospital for the final time with two or three decades of empty days ahead of me. Financially, I'll be secure, but how will I fill my time? It's a thought not worth dwelling on right now, so instead I take a sip from my drink as I decide which group to join. Before I can make up my mind, however, our hostess marches towards me, arms outstretched, a wide smile on her face.

'Freya,' she says, wrapping me in an embrace. When she pulls away, I notice that her pupils are a little dilated; she must have started early. 'I was beginning to worry about you.'

'Oh, I've been here for ages,' I lie.

'See over there?' she says, pointing towards a table bearing the weight of dozens of gift-wrapped presents. 'It's like I'm getting married all over again.'

'Speaking of which,' I say, handing her an envelope that contains a gift voucher to one of the city's most popular restaurants.

'You're very good,' she says. 'But I'll open it later, if you don't mind. You've written your name inside, so I know who it's from?'

'Of course,' I reply. Seated on a banquette a short

distance away, chatting to the head of HR, I notice her husband, Liam, a corporate lawyer who's also due to retire soon; their plan is to backpack around the world together, an ambition that I rather admire. I haven't travelled enough in my life. Perhaps that's something I could do when my time comes. 'I'm going to miss you,' I tell her.

'Ah, you'll have forgotten me by this time next week,' she says, slapping me playfully on the arm. I don't know whether to be offended by this or not, although, if I'm honest, she's not entirely wrong.

'And God knows who they'll stick me with next,' I say. 'We've worked well together, haven't we?'

'We have indeed,' she replies. 'We've always been very professional.' I find this a rather strange response, but perhaps it's appropriate. So many times over the years she's asked me about my life and my relationships outside work, and I've never been very forthcoming, which is probably why she eventually stopped.

My phone buzzes in my pocket and I take it out and look at the screen. *Middlemarch*, it says. We can all use codes to hide our secrets. Louise, looking down, sees the word and frowns.

'Middlemarch,' she says. 'Who or what is Middlemarch?'

'Just a friend,' I tell her. 'No one important.'

'Like the book.'

'Like the book,' I agree.

'And why do you call this friend after a book? What's his name? Or her name?'

I wave away the question. There's simply no way to explain.

'Have you got a fella at last, Freya, is that it?' she asks, looking giddy now, eager for gossip, and I look around in search of an exit. The music is too loud, and I feel claustrophobic. There are too many people here.

'What's he like? Is he good-looking?'

'He's no one,' I repeat. 'Just an acquaintance, that's all.'

'You're a dark horse, I'll give you that. I've often wondered what it is you get up to at night.'

'Believe me,' I say, 'you don't want to know.'

We chat a little more, but she's the star of the night and it's not long before others come over to offer gifts, wish her well and buy her a drink, and I soon lose track of her, thinking that I could probably have one more and then slip away, my duty done. I head towards the bar and am ordering a vodka and cranberry when I hear a voice call my name.

'Dr Petrus!'

I look around and see Aaron seated in a corner booth next to a young woman I don't recognize. He waves me over and, for want of anywhere better to sit, I decide to join them. Unlike the time we went for drinks together, he stands up and kisses me on both cheeks, as if we're old friends.

'Rebecca,' he says to his companion as I sit down, 'this is Dr Petrus. My boss.'

She hesitates noticeably before saying, 'Of course,' and extending a hand towards me. She's neither beautiful nor unattractive, a plain girl whose features would, I think, be difficult to remember afterwards, and I'm a little surprised that Aaron is dating her. Her dark hair is cut short at the cheekbones in an unfashionable attempt at a Louise Brooks bob. Her eyes, however, are quite striking, and when they connect with my own, I feel as if she's reading every thought in my head, which is rather unsettling.

'I've heard a lot about you,' she tells me.

'Dr Petrus, this is my girlfriend, Rebecca,' adds Aaron.

'I told you,' I say. 'When we're not in work, you can just call me Freya. It's nice to meet you, Rebecca. You don't mind being dragged along to one of his work functions, then?'

'Not at all,' she says. 'I haven't met any of his colleagues until tonight and he's spoken so well of Louise.' A slight pause. 'He's talked about you too, of course.'

There's an obvious distinction being made here, but I choose to ignore it. He's probably complained about my attitude towards him on numerous occasions and she's decided to take against me. Not that her opinion matters. I already feel a similar antipathy towards her and guess that she's the dominant force in their relationship. Aaron could do so much better. I drink my vodka more quickly than I should, and before I know it he's taken a fresh order from both of us and disappeared into the crowd. I follow him with my eyes, hoping it won't take him long to be served as I'm not particularly interested in making small talk with this creature.

'So, tell me, Rachel,' I say, 'what is it you do?'

'It's Rebecca,' she says.

'Sorry.'

'And I'm training to be a pilot.'

'Oh yes,' I say, feigning interest. 'Aaron mentioned something about that. I must admit I know nothing about that industry. Are there a lot of female pilots these days?'

'More than you might imagine,' she tells me. 'When I started out, there were fourteen men and three women in the training programme, and now, two years later, only seven of the men are left, but the three of us are still standing.'

'Well, that's something, I suppose. It was the same in medical school. The dropout rate was much higher among the men than the women. Why do you think that is?'

'I couldn't possibly begin to guess,' she says, which shuts that conversation down. Clearly we're not going to bond over the staying power of the sisterhood.

'And was that something you always dreamed of doing?' I ask. 'Since you were a child, I mean?'

'No,' she tells me, glancing at her watch. I consider just sitting back and ignoring her, waiting for her boyfriend to return, but I'm so irritated by her now I feel like this is a challenge that I want to rise to.

'A family thing, perhaps? Was your father a pilot?'

She laughs and shakes her head. The expression on her face is impossible to read. I'm considering asking whether she always behaves this rudely towards complete strangers when my phone buzzes again. I feel a stab of irritation as I take it out and look at the screen.

I want to come over.

Not tonight, I reply quickly. *I'm going into surgery. My phone will be off for the next few hours.*

'Something important?' asks Rebecca, and I shrug.

'Something I need to take care of, certainly,' I tell her. 'I just have to figure out how.'

'I'm sure you will.'

'I'm sure I will. You have something between your teeth, by the way.'

She doesn't, but I rather enjoy watching her suck at her gums, trying to extract whatever it is.

'Your accent,' I say. 'You're Irish?'

'Yes.'

'Did you know Louise before, then?'

She stares at me as if I'm the stupidest woman alive. 'No, of course not,' she says. 'There are five million people in Ireland. We don't all know each other.'

Thankfully, before I can tell her to go fuck herself, Aaron returns and places the drinks on the table, glancing from his girlfriend to me and back again. It's a strange moment. I almost feel as if I'm being interviewed to join a coven, or being told the reasons why I'm being excluded from one.

'I was just asking Rachel,' I say, 'whether she—'

'Rebecca,' says Rebecca, for the second time.

Naturally, I know her name is Rebecca. I'm getting it wrong deliberately just to demonstrate to her how unimportant she is to me.

'I'm so sorry,' I say. 'Rebecca, of course. I was just asking Rebecca whether her father was a pilot.'

They turn to look at each other and he retreats slightly in his seat. To my surprise, she leans towards him and they kiss. I turn away, noticing that not only are they

JOHN BOYNE

holding hands but that they're clasping them very tightly, their knuckles whitening against the skin. My aversion towards him, which had diminished in recent times, immediately returns. I find their behaviour both boorish and disrespectful.

'How about you?' asks Rebecca, turning back to me when she's finished molesting the poor boy. 'Were your parents surgeons?'

'No,' I say. 'My mother was an architect, and my father was a mathematics professor in Cambridge.'

Something in Rebecca's expression tells me that she doesn't believe a word of this and, of course, she'd be right not to.

'Are they still alive?'

'No, they died in a house fire when I was twelve.'

Aaron raises an eyebrow. 'You never told me that,' he says.

'Why would I?'

'But a house fire. Is that why you . . . the burns unit, I mean?'

I try to recall whether I ever gave him a reason why I made this my speciality. He did ask me about it on our quasi-date, I recall, but I can't remember what I said and am anxious about contradicting myself.

'It played a part in it,' I tell him. 'But not the only part.'

'Was it arson?' asks Rebecca.

'That's a strange assumption,' I say, turning to her. 'Wouldn't an accident be the more likely explanation?'

'It would, yes. But was it?'

'No, faulty wiring,' I say after a pause. 'A spark in the

garage where the fuse box was located ignited a dozen cans of paint. We were having the house renovated at the time. Putting in a pool, among other things.'

'How awful.'

'It was, yes.'

'But you escaped unharmed.'

'I was staying with a friend that night,' I tell her. 'Otherwise, I would have died too.'

'And did they catch whoever did it?'

'No one did it,' I say, raising my voice a little. 'I told you, it was an accident.'

'I mean, did they arrest whoever installed the wiring? Surely there'd be a case for manslaughter?'

I stare at her, baffled by her prying. I'm not prepared to discuss this any longer, not least because the more lies I tell, the more difficult they are to remember.

'You never answered my question,' I say.

'What question was that?'

'I asked what your father did. Or does.'

She doesn't hesitate for a moment.

'He was the head of the National Swimming Federation in Ireland,' she tells me. 'He held that position for many years until it was discovered that he'd sexually abused eight young girls in his care. Eight that we know of, anyway. There was a trial. Quite a famous one in Ireland, actually. And he went to prison. He's still there, in fact.'

I'm astonished by the frankness of this admission. She reaches for her glass and takes a drink.

'I see,' I say, a rather impotent response on my part,

but I can't quite think what else to say. 'That must have been very painful for you.'

'It was, yes.'

'And are you still in contact with him?'

She shakes her head. 'Of course not. Why would I be?'

'Well, I presume you loved him once.'

'When I was a child. But now? No. I wake every day hoping to learn of his death. I'll never speak to Brendan again,' she adds, and I notice she refers to him by his first name, as I always did with Hannah and Beth, removing all sense of familial connection. 'Anyone who hurts a child forfeits all rights, in my opinion.'

'Did he admit his guilt?' I ask. 'Or was it a jury trial?'

'Why do you ask?'

'Because I'm interested. I served on a jury myself once.'

'To this day he refuses to take any responsibility for his actions. His victims have to live with it though. Well, some of them, anyway.'

'Some of them? What do you mean?'

'That there must be some who are dead. Girls who took their own lives.'

An image flashes into my mind.

Rufus seated by the side of my bed, barefoot and trembling.

Rufus on the gurney as it was wheeled into A&E, the purple bruises around his neck from where his school tie had choked him.

'I admire how willing you are to talk about this,' I tell her. 'Utterly unashamed.'

'Why would I be ashamed? I didn't hurt anyone. Don't you think it's the perpetrator who should feel shame?'

'Of course I do. But I suppose—'

'You suppose what?'

'Well, just from an intellectual standpoint, one has to wonder what happened to your father to make him do the things he did.'

'Does one?' she asks, stressing the *one*, as if I'm condescending to her. 'Why?'

'In order to understand it.'

'It's not something I want to understand.'

'Then how do we, as a society, learn from it? How do we stop it from happening again?'

'I don't give a fuck about society,' she replies. 'I only care about the lives he destroyed. Those girls' lives, first and foremost. And my sister's. And my mother's. And mine.'

'Of course,' I say. 'Look, I'm a surgeon, not a psychologist, but these things interest me, that's all. And the fact that you're so up front about what your father did makes me—'

'It's quite simple really,' she says. 'Brendan was – is – a paedophile.'

'But do you think he was born that way or that something happened to him, somewhere in his own youth, that led him to do the things he did?'

She hesitates now. I don't know how long she's been struggling with her family history, but it's clear that I'm asking her something she's never properly considered before.

'It's not impossible,' she says after a lengthy pause, her words coming out carefully, as if she's judging the weight of each one, 'that he was born with the sort of brain that meant that, one day, he would find himself sexually attracted to children. That can happen, I suppose. But surely the difference comes in the decision whether or not to act upon those urges. Right and wrong comes into it. A man – even a woman, for that matter – might have such impulses. But because most of us are moral human beings who don't set out to hurt others, we do nothing to feed them. We never would. Can a person be blamed for how they were born? No, of course not. But it's neither here nor there, is it? It's the committing of the act that matters. A man, a regular heterosexual man, might have rape fantasies that he cannot control in his imagination but that he would never in a trillion years indulge. None of us can be held responsible for the things that lurk in the darkest parts of our minds. But in our lives? Yes, we can. So whether something happened to Brendan when he was a child or not, I genuinely do not fucking care, Freya. If it did, he could have chosen to break the cycle. If it didn't, he could have chosen not to start one. But he *did* do what he did. He made that decision. So fuck him. Let him rot. I'll open a bottle of champagne when he dies.'

A lengthy silence ensues, and I glance at Aaron, who has remained silent throughout this exchange, but he's looking at the floor, his brow furrowed. The resulting awkwardness is broken by Louise approaching us and, in her drunken state, planting a kiss on my left cheek and one on Aaron's right, before insisting on taking a photograph of the three of us on her smartphone.

'I knew you two would get along in the end,' she says, and Aaron smiles back at her.

'We're not quite there yet,' he says.

13

IT WAS THE FINAL days of my stay in Cornwall. Since the
night they buried me alive, Arthur and Pascoe had been
reluctant to spend much time with me, no doubt worried
that I might hold them to account for what they had done.
Instead, I chose not to mention it at all, hoping they'd
think that I'd either forgotten about it entirely or had
experienced no traumatic effects. Only once, when Pascoe
brought it up in a way that made it clear that the twins had
rehearsed this conversation, did we even touch upon it.

'That was a stupid thing you did that night,' he said as
we walked along the beach, the two boys to my right
with me by the water's edge, for they never allowed me
to stand between them.

'What night?' I asked.

'You know what night. Climbing into the box like that.
Sleeping in it. You might have died.'

A lengthy silence ensued. So this, I told myself, was the
way that they had decided to frame what had happened.
As my fault.

'I know,' I said at last, keeping my tone steady. 'Thank
you, both of you, for saving me. I don't know what I'd
have done if you hadn't.'

Immediately, the tension between us seemed to dissipate, and I watched as they gave each other reassuring smiles. Perhaps they genuinely thought I was so stupid that I actually believed this version of events.

'You're just a kid,' said Arthur, ignoring the fact that, if I was, then he had spent much of the summer raping a child. 'But you need to be more careful in the future. Especially when you go home, because we won't be there to protect you.'

Later, in the village, I ran into Eli, who was sitting outside a pub with a beer, reading a newspaper and smoking a cigarette. I waved to him and he called me over, inviting me to sit down. He asked me how I was, and I told him the truth, that I missed him.

'Miss you too, sweetheart,' he said, folding his paper and putting it to one side. 'But your mum, she gave me the old heave-ho.'

'Why?' I asked, interested to know, as it had seemed to me that she'd been lucky to find someone as nice as him.

He rubbed his thumb and index finger together.

'Money,' he said. 'I don't have enough for her, do I? She's got a few good years left in her yet and she's throwing the line out, hoping to reel in a bigger fish.' He took a drag from his cigarette and stared off in the direction of the sea before shaking his head. 'Forget I said that,' he said, turning back to me with a smile. 'She's your mum. I shouldn't say anything bad about her to you.'

'She gave birth to me,' I told him. 'But that's about it. She's not my mum really.'

'I never did understand why she gave you up,' he said,

and I repeated the hand gesture he had made to me –
money – which made him laugh.

'Still, she was just a teenager, I suppose,' he said. 'Can't
blame her for not being ready. I don't hold grudges. We
had fun together, but neither of us saw it as anything
long term. Truth is, I'm not the kind of guy who gets
upset about things like that. If someone wants to be with
me, great. And if they don't, well, I'm not gonna lose any
sleep over it.'

In my mind, I returned to my earlier fantasy that he
would marry Beth and adopt me, only this time I didn't
want her in the picture at all. I wanted it to be just the
two of us.

'When are you going home?' he asked.

'Day after tomorrow.'

'Shame,' he said. 'I'll miss you.'

I felt myself light up from within.

'We could do something together before I go,' I suggested, and he raised an eyebrow, looking slightly baffled.

'Like what?'

'I dunno. Have dinner. Somewhere fancy though, not
just down the pub for cod and chips and mushy peas. I
can get that any time.'

He shook his head. 'Don't think that would be right,'
he said.

'It doesn't really have to be somewhere fancy. I was
only joking. The local is as good as anywhere.'

'Still,' he said, looking away and glancing at his watch.
'Probably not.'

I felt embarrassed and confused and worried that he

was going to leave. I'm just like her, amn't I, I thought.
Just like Beth. And I'll end up just like her too.

'Why did Mr Teague fire you?' I asked, anxious to
change the subject.

'Because he's an idiot.'

'No, but why?'

'Doesn't want to spend the cash,' he said. 'Happy to
throw it away on sofas, massive televisions and sound
systems, but he wants all the behind-the-scenes shit done
on the cheap. That's what rich people are like, Freya.
Tight as fuck.'

'What behind-the-scenes stuff?' I asked.

'Electrics,' he said. 'Cheap cables. Cheap plumbing.
Looks good on the outside, but when things go wrong,
and they will sooner or later, it'll be a shitshow. Still,' he
said, taking a long drink from his beer, 'it's his money. If
he wants to throw it away, that's on him. But it's a . . .
what's the phrase? . . . a false economy. Ten years from
now – five – he'll be pulling everything out and having to
start all over again.'

'You won't do it for him then, will you?'

''Course I will,' he said, breaking into a wide smile.
'Work's work and a pay packet's a pay packet. If he wants
me to redo that house every few years for the rest of my
life, I'm good with it, as long as he pays me.'

He reached for his cigarette pack, removed another,
and looked around for his lighter. He stood up, went over
to the next table and asked for a match from another cus-
tomer, while I retrieved his lighter from where it had
dropped underneath the bench and put it in my pocket.

When he came back, I'd moved around to his side of the table and was sitting in the seat next to his. He seemed a little surprised by this, but I explained that the sun had been in my eyes.

'Can I have a drink?' I asked.

'Sure,' he said. 'What do you want?'

I racked my brain for things I'd heard Beth or Hannah order over the years and asked for a vodka and cranberry. Eli threw his head back and laughed.

'I meant a Coke or a Fanta,' he said. 'You're twelve years old.'

'I'll be thirteen in November,' I told him.

'So come back to me in November five years from now and I'll get you one then.'

I gave in and let him buy me a Sprite, and when he returned, carrying another beer for himself, I set aside the straw and glass he'd brought with him and decided to drink it directly from the bottle, just as he was doing.

'You're better off without her anyway,' I told him, doing my best to sound grown up.

'Without who?'

'Without Beth. You're too good for her.'

He smiled and shrugged. 'She's a piece of work, that's for sure.'

'I mean it. I've met lots of her boyfriends over the years, and I've hated them all. But you're different.'

'Cheers.'

'Do you know the caves down by the beach?'

'Sure,' he said. 'Why?'

'Just asking. I'd like to visit them again before I go.'

'Tide'll be in soon. You better wait till tomorrow morning.'

'We could go together then.'

He shook his head and took a drag from his cigarette. 'Sorry, kid,' he said. 'Starting a new job tomorrow. A smaller house than the Teagues', but I know the owner and he's all right. It'll be simple enough.'

'Don't call me that,' I said quietly.

'What?'

'I'm not a kid.'

'All right,' he replied. 'I didn't mean anything by it.'

'I know you didn't,' I told him, reaching out my right hand and placing it on his left leg, close to his crotch, as I moved my face closer to his.

I had expected some sort of reaction – this was, after all, how Arthur and Pascoe liked to begin things with me – but I hadn't expected what happened next. It was as if he'd received an electric shock. He leapt from the seat, knocking over both our drinks and his chair, jumped back and stared at me wide-eyed.

'What the fuck?' he said.

I stared back at him, confused by his response.

'I really like you, Eli,' I said.

'Jesus, Freya,' he said, running his hands through his hair and looking around to make sure no one was watching us. 'You're just a child. I didn't . . . I wasn't trying to . . .' He looked both frightened and upset. 'That's absolutely not what I'm looking for,' he told me. 'I've just tried to be a friend to you, that's all. Christ, I hope you haven't thought that I . . . that I've been trying to . . .'

He seemed so distraught that I looked away, already bored by him. Clearly, I'd made another mistake. I'd hoped he might take me away from Hannah, from Beth, from the twins. That he might be a father to me, or a dad, or a brother, or a lover. Anything. Someone who would love me. But no. He was just another person who didn't care about me in the slightest.

I stood up and walked towards him as he backed away.

'You can relax,' I told him. 'You're an old man, you're nothing special, and I have no interest in Beth's cast-offs.'

I turned away then. I only saw him once more, at his trial a year later, when I sat at the back of the courtroom and watched him collapse in the dock when the verdict was delivered.

Served him right.

I was due to get the train back to Norfolk on Saturday morning, and Beth had promised that we would spend Friday night together, presumably to make up for the fact that we had barely spent any time together since my arrival. She'd seen me at breakfast, and occasionally before I went to bed, but had barely acknowledged my presence outside of that. Even on her days off, she either stayed in bed until the late afternoon, or lay on the sofa watching rubbish TV and sending me to the village to buy food and cigarettes.

Although she promised to take me to the pub with her for dinner, I knew she'd find a reason to cancel. Kitto had been coming to ours, or she'd been going to his, almost every night for the last week and it made me laugh to think that she actually believed he was grooming her to become the mistress of the big house, like some Victorian housemaid who manages to snare the wealthy widowed duke. True to form, she told me that we'd have breakfast together on Saturday instead, giving me four pounds to go to the local burger shop for my dinner and telling me that she wouldn't be home because Mr Teague was taking her to the pub, the one where she'd supposedly been going to take me, and afterwards she'd be spending the night in his house.

I waited until late, long past one o'clock in the morning, when I saw the lights go on, and watched from the safety of the beach as Beth and Kitto returned home. Upstairs, where Arthur and Pascoe slept, remained unfinished, but downstairs was almost completed. They might have been any wealthy couple coming back from a night out together. I made my way closer, past the pit where the swimming pool would never, in fact, be installed, and watched as they stood in the kitchen, opening a bottle of wine and kissing. At one point, he pressed her up against the fridge and his hand disappeared beneath her dress. When he went to the bathroom, I watched as Beth opened cupboards, examining their contents, then looked around the room, taking everything in, probably deluding herself into imagining the changes she would make when she won her upgrade. And I continued to watch when, eventually, the lights went off and they went upstairs to the bedroom.

Another hour passed before I risked entering. It wasn't

difficult to get in. Eli had keys to the property and he'd left them at Beth's when he was dismissed from his dual positions as site foreman and boyfriend. Making my way upstairs, I carefully opened the door to the master bedroom and looked in at Beth and Kitto, who were sleeping side by side, their mouths wide open, looking ugly as they dreamed of wildly different futures. Then I went to the twins' room and stood over them. They were curled up together, Arthur's arms wrapped around Pascoe's naked torso. Leaning down, I placed a gentle kiss on both their foreheads, and they moved only slightly beneath the covers before settling back into place.

Returning downstairs, I went into the garage, where the fuse box was located, along with a dozen cans of paint and various flammable materials. From my pocket, I took out Eli's lighter, holding it in a handkerchief so my fingerprints wouldn't overwrite his, and found a bottle of methylated spirits, which I splashed around the floor. Pulling a few wires from the fuses, I lit one, and it connected quickly, igniting others, before feasting on the flammable liquid on the floor. I stepped away, watching as it burst into life. It was a beautiful sight to behold. With all the work going on in the house, I knew it wouldn't take long for the woodwork to soak up the blaze and spread towards the second floor. They'd never know, any of them. They do say that it's not the house fire that kills people, it's the smoke. All four of them would be dead before their bodies were cremated. They wouldn't feel a thing.

Before returning to the cottage, I made sure to drop

the lighter in the grass, somewhere a little hidden but easy enough for the police to find. Eli deserved this. He could have saved me but had chosen not to, so he could take his punishment too.

I slept well that night, even through the sounds of the sirens from outside, which proved a good thing, as the next few days were busy as people sympathized and took care of me. The police asked whether Eli had ever touched me, and I said no, because I knew he'd be going to jail for the rest of his life anyway so didn't feel the need to add to his charges. Soon I was taken back to Norfolk, and back to Hannah, and we lived together till I was eighteen. During those years I devoted myself to my schoolwork because I knew the only way out was to win a scholarship, which, in time, I did. I'm pretty sure I said goodbye on the morning I left. And that was that. I was gone.

She's probably still alive, somewhere. After all, she'll only be in her sixties. But Beth is gone. And Kitto Teague is gone.

And most importantly, Arthur and Pascoe, those two malevolent fourteen-year-olds, never made it to fifteen, and never got to hurt anyone again.

14

THE RESOLUTION TO WHAT I have come to think of as
my Middlemarch problem arrives more easily than
I expected.

George texts me on Sunday following Louise's retirement party, demanding sex, as usual. I tell him it won't
be possible, that I have a complicated surgery scheduled
for the following morning. A four-year-old child whose
legs were badly burned when a deep-fat fryer fell on him
from a kitchen counter. (Which is actually true.) He
grumbles a bit but, showing a little decency at last,
accepts this.

He messages again the following evening. I ignore his
text and set my alarm for the fairly random time of
1.13 a.m., at which point I briefly wake and send an
already-typed reply to explain that I've been in the hospital all night and didn't have my phone with me, but that
I'm longing for him and want to see him soon.

On Tuesday afternoon, he tells me that he wants to
come over at seven o'clock, but once again I don't reply. I
have a plan in place, but I need to wait until Wednesday,
which is always the quietest night at work.

Annoyed by my silence, he texts later to say that, as

much as he'd like to hook up with me later in the week, he won't be able to, because there's a girl called Holly in his year and they're going to a film together, and he'll probably fuck her afterwards, so I've missed out, and I'm going to spend every day for the rest of my life regretting that I lost him, but I have no one to blame but myself.

I don't reply.

Thirty-four minutes later, he texts to tell me that Holly doesn't exist, that he made her up, that he loves me and only me, and that eleven months from now, when he turns sixteen, we can get married, and that he'll do anything I ask of him if we can just meet up.

I don't reply.

Seventeen minutes later he texts to tell me that he's going to report me to the police for having sex with him when he was underage. He's planning on taking me to court and making sure that I'm sent to prison, then suing me for ten million pounds for emotional distress.

I don't reply.

Eight minutes later, he sends me a dick pic.

I don't reply.

Fourteen minutes later, he tells me that he's really sorry for everything he's said so far, it's just that he knows that he and I are meant to be together, like in that film *Romeo and Juliet*.

I don't reply.

Two minutes later, he tells me to go fuck myself.

I don't reply.

Eighteen minutes later, he tells me that the only reason he fucked me was because he felt sorry for me.

I don't reply.

Thirty seconds later, he tells me I'm a prick tease.

I don't reply.

Seven minutes later, he tells me that a teacher in school called Miss Woods blew him in the art room during first break.

I don't reply.

Eleven minutes later, he sends me a video holding the second and third fingers of his right hand in front of his mouth, his tongue pushing through.

I don't reply.

Four minutes later, he tells me he's going to tell his dad everything.

I don't reply.

Twelve minutes later, he sends me a link to a YouTube video of Billie Eilish singing 'Bad Guy' and says this is his favourite song of all time.

I don't reply.

Six minutes later, he asks whether I've watched the latest season of *The Summer I Turned Pretty*.

I don't reply.

Nine minutes later, he says he's always wanted to go to Venice and maybe we can go there over the summer.

I don't reply.

Twenty-one minutes later, he tells me that I'm a paedophile and I should be castrated, which is too baffling a suggestion to even consider replying to.

Six minutes later, he tells me that he's never loved anyone as much as he loves me.

I don't reply.

Thirty seconds later, he tells me that I'm an incredible person and I should stop running. (I have no idea what I'm supposedly running from.)

I don't reply.

Five minutes later, he tells me that if I don't call him, he's going to take a taxi to the American embassy, then run as fast as he can towards the guards standing outside holding his PlayStation controller in his hands, and they'll be so freaked out that they'll probably shoot him dead.

I don't reply.

Nine minutes later, he sends me a video of a dog whose master has come back from serving in Afghanistan and the dog goes completely crazy when he sees him. *I love dogs but I don't have one*, he tells me.

I don't reply.

Four minutes later, he says he's about to take a piss and can we FaceTime while he does it.

I don't reply.

Eight minutes later, he tells me he's going into the hospital tomorrow to report me.

I don't reply.

Twenty minutes later, he says he's just ordered a Deliveroo. Chicken nuggets, cheese-loaded chips and a Sprite.

I don't reply.

Nine minutes later, he tells me he's been watching Joe Fazer videos online and do I think he should work out more and build bigger muscles like Joe, who, he tells me, is inspirational.

I don't reply.

Fifteen minutes later, he tells me that if I was with him right now, he would strangle me with his bare hands.

I don't reply.

Twenty seconds later, he tells me that when he kills me, it will be painful, it will be with a knife, that he'll stab me slowly, repeatedly, pushing the knife in and out of different parts of my body, and he'll get away with it too, because he's too clever to get caught.

I don't reply.

Four minutes later, he asks me which female movie star I'd fuck if I had the chance.

I don't reply.

Seven minutes later, he says that if it was the other way round, he'd fuck Penn Badgley.

I don't reply.

Nine minutes later, he tells me that he was only joking, he's not gay.

I don't reply.

Twelve minutes later, he tells me that he doesn't mean there's anything wrong with being gay, that one of his best friends has already come out and he's cool with it, but it's not something he'd be into himself.

I don't reply.

Eight minutes later, he tells me he's thinking of reading *The Mill on the Floss*, so he'll have something to talk about when people mention his name.

I don't reply.

Six minutes later, he says he's stoned.

I don't reply.

Two minutes later, he tells me that he's not stoned at

all, that he was just making that up to impress me. He asks whether I remember him refusing my offer of a cigarette on that 'incredible' day when we first met.

I don't reply.

Seven minutes later, he tells me that he thinks there's something wrong with him because he's never not horny.

I don't reply.

One minute later, he tells me that I'm a cunt.

I don't reply.

Eighteen minutes later, he tells me that I mean absolutely nothing to him, that he's had a lot better.

I don't reply.

Three minutes later, he asks what's it like to be a frigid bitch.

I don't reply.

Four minutes later, he tells me that I'm obviously a lesbian.

I don't reply.

Eight minutes later, he says that he's thinking of getting a tattoo of my name on his arm.

I don't reply.

Ten seconds later, he asks can he come over.

I don't reply.

One minute later, he tells me that if I don't answer his call, he's going to phone the *Daily Mail* and tell them how he was sexually abused by an old woman.

I don't reply.

Seven minutes later, he sends me a photo of a ham, cheese and onion toastie he's just made. *Just call me Gordon Ramsay!* he adds.

I don't reply.

Eleven minutes later, he tells me he's thinking of signing up for the army when he turns sixteen, even though his dad wants him to take his A levels and then go on to uni.

I don't reply.

Four minutes later, he asks me what the fuck are the royal family all about? Like, it's 2024.

I don't reply.

Two minutes later, he asks me whether it's difficult being so fat and ugly.

I don't reply.

Nine minutes later, he says that in his film studies class in school they're watching *Death in Venice* and have I seen it? It's, like, a hundred years old, he tells me, but it's pretty good. Last week, they watched *Chinatown*, which he says was fucked up. He's not sure, but he thinks the dad had sex with the daughter, but it was too confusing and there were no action scenes other than when some little French guy slit the main guy's nose open with a knife. *You're a very nosey fellow, kitty-cat, the French guy said. That's how I think of you, Freya. My kitty-cat.*

I don't reply.

Thirteen minutes later, he says he feels sorry for my patients because I must be the worst doctor in the history of the universe and anyone I treat will probably die.

I don't reply.

Two minutes later, he tells me I have cellulite all over my face.

I don't reply, but at least this makes me laugh.

Eight minutes later, he says he's going to sleep, that he's tired, but that he loves me.

I don't reply.

One minute later, he texts:

Talk tomorrow, luv ya sexy x

I don't reply.

When the night of the long texts finally comes to an end, I realize I have no choice. I can't allow this to continue any longer.

They say that the easiest way to hide something is to do it in plain sight. Which is what I do. The following evening, I message to apologize for not responding to any of his messages, telling him I had an emergency surgery, turned my phone off, and just fell into bed exhausted when I got home. I feel the same way, I tell him. That the age difference between us doesn't matter. That he's the best lover I've ever had. That when I look to the future, all I see is me and him together. That I only want to be with him. And then, finally, I tell him that I want him to come to my flat at nine o'clock tonight and that I'll make it up to him for keeping him waiting so long.

He replies with a series of indecipherable emojis that I don't have the energy to translate into English, but I assume they mean he's pleased by my suggestion, then throw my phone on the sofa, make some pasta, listen to some music, do some prep for an operation coming up three days later, and wait for him to arrive.

'Hi, bae,' he says when I open the front door, and it takes every ounce of my willpower not to rip his throat out right then.

'Beer?' I ask.

'I'm not in the mood for a beer,' he says. 'Do you have any Jack Daniel's?'

'Sure,' I say.

'I'd, like, literally kill for a JD,' he says.

I try not to laugh at his utter absurdity and make my way towards the kitchen.

'How do you like it?' I shout, as if he's a whisky connoisseur.

'On the rocks,' he says, and I wonder does he even know what that means. I pour a healthy measure into the glass, add some ice, then a substantial amount of the oxycodone and morphine I lifted from the hospital's dispensary earlier, before bringing it out to him.

'I'm sorry about all those messages,' he says, looking a little embarrassed. 'I was just . . . having a bad night, that's all.'

'Don't worry about it,' I say, smiling. 'I was flattered. They made me realize how much you like me.'

'I don't just *like* you,' he says, and I notice that he's sipping his whisky in tiny amounts so he doesn't have to actually taste any of it. I need him to actually drink it. 'I *love* you, Freya.'

'And I love you, George,' I say.

He beams.

'We're really going to make this happen, aren't we?' he asks.

'Absolutely,' I say. 'It's time to tell people. Your dad. Your mum. Your friends. Everyone.'

'They're gonna lose their fucking minds,' he says.

JOHN BOYNE

He tries for another sip of his Jack Daniel's, but he's losing the battle.

'Oh wait,' I say, standing up. 'I forgot the Coke.'

'What?'

'No one drinks Jack Daniel's straight,' I tell him. 'You need some Coke in it.'

I reach out to take his glass, and he nods. 'Yeah, I didn't wanna say,' he replies, looking relieved.

I go to the kitchen and open the fridge, where my trusty cans of Coke are waiting for me, and pour a decent amount into his glass.

When I hand it back to him, he sips it cautiously, but the Coke overpowers the taste of both the whisky and the opioids, and he makes much better progress now.

It only takes about thirty minutes before he starts to have difficulty breathing and then, as I watch, he falls to the ground and suffers a stroke. I do a little work on my laptop, answering a few emails and updating some events on my calendar as he stares at me in terror. His eyes are focused on mine, consumed by fear, but I do nothing to help him. As it happens, I become so involved with the case studies I'm reading that I don't even notice when he dies.

A doctor wearing a white coat and carrying the appropriate lanyard can get through any door in the hospital. I've worked there for years. I know where the CCTV cameras are and where they're not. I know the circuitous if rather convoluted journey I can take to wheel a gurney from the loading bay into one of the service elevators and bring it to the morgue, where there are thirty cold lockers, only half of which are ever occupied, without fear of my actions being recorded.

When George's body is eventually discovered, no one will have the slightest clue who he is or how he got there.

When I get home, I scrub the flat clean of his presence and have a drink myself, finishing the bottle of whisky. This whole experience, coupled with what happened with Rufus, has forced me to rethink my lifestyle completely. How many boys' lives have I ruined, anyway? A hundred? Two hundred? That's probably enough.

Maybe it's time to stop.

15

Since my twelfth summer, I have been consumed by fire, laying waste to everything and everyone around me. Today, when I wake, things feel different. Enough has happened. Too many risks have been taken. It's time to quench the flames for ever and find some form of peace.

I've taken a week's holiday, and it feels strange to return to the hospital and for Louise not to be there. Her replacement is a nurse around my own age, Michael, who I don't know terribly well but with whom I've never had any issues, so I resolve to stay positive in the hope that we can build a relationship as strong as the one that she and I enjoyed. He's waiting for me when I exit the staircase on the sixth floor, today's files in his hands.

'Good morning, Dr Petrus,' he says, offering something that resembles a slight bow. There's no coffee or KitKat, but I can train him on this.

'Good morning, Michael,' I say. 'And welcome to your first day in your new role.'

He smiles and acknowledges this, holding the files out for me.

'In future,' I tell him, 'you can just give these to Aaron

or whatever intern I'm lumbered with at the time. My preference is that they're laid out on my desk when I arrive every day.'

'Of course,' he says. 'And just so I know, how much longer will Dr Umber be on rotation with you?'

'Two more weeks, I think. After that, I'll be running solo for a few months before they inflict someone else on me.'

I take the files and head down the corridor towards my office. Once inside, I place them on my desk and turn on the computer, feeling a sense of calm. George's body was discovered in the morgue early last week, and, as expected, no one has been able to figure out how it got there, although his father had reported him missing to the police. They eventually put two and two together and he was identified by his mother that same evening. An investigation has been launched, but everyone is completely baffled as to what took place. Naturally, I'm steering clear of it all, and I'm certain there's nothing that can trace him back to me. I wiped his phone back to factory settings before removing the SIM card, then incinerated both. One last fire.

As for Rufus, well, he's survived much longer than I expected. In fact, rather annoyingly, he's still alive. However, there's no brain activity and the hospital wants to turn his life support off, but his mother is fighting this, unable to accept that her son is, in real terms, already dead. Apparently, she's hired a lawyer to ensure that the boy's machine is kept on.

It's late afternoon and I'm checking on one of my

post-operative patients when Aaron appears at the door
to the ward. He's been absent all morning, which is unlike
him, but I've grown more tolerant of his presence these
days and decide not to reproach him. Instead, I offer him
that very rare thing – a smile – although he doesn't
reciprocate.

'Dr Petrus,' he says. 'I wonder could we talk privately?
In your office?'

I'm a little surprised by his tone, which is rather serious, but I nod and tell him of course, that he can go
there now if he wants, and I'll follow in a moment. I
watch as he makes his way down the corridor, and I go to
the bottled-water machine for something to drink. I have
a strange premonition that the conversation ahead of us
will be an uncomfortable one.

I wait a few minutes before following him and, once
inside, I'm surprised to find him standing by the window,
staring out, which seems rather audacious instead of sitting opposite my desk. I have to press past him to get to
my own chair and he's almost surly as he steps away. I
point to the chair and, almost reluctantly, he sits.

'So,' I say, glancing towards my computer screen and
moving the mouse to make it seem like I'm simply too
busy to give him my full attention. 'You wanted to talk?'

'Yes,' he says. 'You know I only have two weeks left,
right?'

'I do. I hope your time here has proved interesting and
educational?'

'It has.' He pauses for a moment. 'You're a very fine
doctor.'

I acknowledge this with a slight nod of my head. 'Thank you,' I say.

'I mean it,' he continues. 'Probably the best I've worked with on any of my rotations. You're efficient, quick to diagnose, although you don't rush to judgement. You show great compassion towards your patients. It's one of the things that I find so contradictory about you, Freya. You're quite a complex individual, really, aren't you?'

I frown. Am I? Perhaps I am. But I don't really have any interest in a character analysis from him. I choose not to react to his use of my first name at work.

'We all are, I suppose,' I reply. 'Is this what you wanted to talk to me about, Aaron? I mean, I appreciate your kind words, but—'

'No, I wanted to talk to you about the Rozelli Programme.'

I sit back in surprise. This is the last thing I expected.

'Oh, right,' I say. 'If you're going to tell me that my talk in your school is what made you interested in becoming a doctor, then you've told me that already.'

'No, it's not that,' he says, shaking his head.

'You want to take part in the programme? I can certainly put you in touch with the facilitator. But, to be honest, they usually want people a little more advanced in their careers. Although I don't particularly see why that has to be the case. I'm sure you could—'

'I don't want to take part in it,' he says. 'I was a student on it, remember?'

'Yes,' I say, growing weary now. 'Look, Aaron, what's all this about?'

'You came to our school. You made medicine sound like a vocation.'

'It is a vocation,' I reply.

'You said that every day doctors and nurses save lives. That it's the most important job in the world.'

'I still think that.'

'I was very, very shy back then, but I was so inspired by the things you said that I plucked up all my courage to talk to you afterwards. You were kind to me. Encouraging.' He takes a deep breath, as if he's been holding this in for a long time. 'I was only fourteen years old at the time.'

I stare at him. Something stirs inside me and I feel a slight pain in the pit of my stomach. From the day he arrived, I knew there was something I didn't like about him, something that made me deeply uncomfortable in his presence, but I could never quite put my finger on what it was.

'Do you remember the night we went for a drink together?' he continues. 'At one point, I started laughing. Because of the song that was playing.'

'I have no idea what you're talking about,' I say.

' "You don't remember me, do you?" ' he sings quietly in a rather tuneful voice.

'I'm glad I was helpful to you,' I say.

'Oh, you were the polar opposite of helpful,' he says.

I look down at my desk. The screensaver on my computer screen has kicked in and, as it always does, a random word from the dictionary, with its definition, is scrolling across the screen.

Element: One of the four basic building blocks of matter.

'I don't know why you're telling me all this,' I say, and he shakes his head.

'Yes, you do,' he replies. 'I can see from the expression on your face that you do. Please don't play the innocent. It's sort of pathetic.'

'I don't know what you think you remember,' I say, and he raises a hand to silence me. For the first time since his arrival in the hospital, I obey him without question.

'I remember everything,' he says. 'Every minute of that evening. How you told me that you had some textbooks that were suitable for boys my age who were interested in a career in medicine. You offered to loan them to me. I was so excited. You said they were back in your flat, but you could drive me there and lend them to me.'

'Just stop,' I say.

'It all seemed fine. Exciting, even. You were treating me like an adult. And you were so hot.' He laughs a little. 'I mean, you still are.'

'Aaron.'

'But then we got to your flat and there were no text-books, were there? You gave me a can of Coke. Do you remember that? And when I opened it, it exploded all over me. I was soaked. You made me get undressed. You said you'd wash my T-shirt. The next thing I knew, I was in your bed.'

What does he want from me? Money? That can be arranged.

'Did you object?' I ask coolly. 'Or did you enjoy it?'

He pauses and considers this.

'I enjoyed it in the moment,' he tells me. 'But then I

was just a child. Only fourteen. It didn't take long for me to feel that I'd done something wrong. Something I wasn't ready for. Within a few months, I'd changed completely. I felt I'd lost something I wasn't ready to lose. And I don't mean the obvious. I mean something far deeper. My innocence, I suppose. My childhood.'

He takes a long, deep breath, as if he's been waiting a long time to say this phrase, which, I suppose, he has.

'You raped me, Freya.'

A mixture of fear and horror runs through my body when he uses this word.

'Don't be so melodramatic,' I tell him. 'It's obscene that you would use that word for something in which you were entirely complicit.'

'I don't know if you care about this or not, but I wasn't able to have a normal relationship for years. Even now, with Rebecca, things aren't quite as they should be. Sexually, I mean. Because of you. Because of what you did to me. The funny thing is, I still wanted to be a doctor,' he continues, looking towards the window. 'So I went to university, studied medicine and, in time, tracked you down. I wanted to learn more about you. To see you in action. To understand what kind of person would do something like that to a child. Before I—'

'Before you what?'

'Before I go to the police.'

There's a lengthy silence. But I'm not ready to concede just yet.

'And you honestly think they'll believe you?' I ask.

'Who knows? But they'll be obliged to investigate it. I

told my best friend at the time. And we've talked about it on and off over the years. He's willing to give evidence. I think you know him, actually.'

'How would I know your best friend?' I ask, utterly baffled by this.

'And I can't have been the only person you did it to, can I? There must be others. I assume the police have some way of exploring that. Once they start, who knows how many will come out of the woodwork.'

'You have no idea what they did to me,' I say.

'Who?' he asks, frowning. 'What who did to you?'

'The twins.'

He stares at me blankly.

'Do you want money?' I ask, knowing what his answer will be.

'Christ, no,' he says. 'I don't want a penny from you. That's kind of insulting, actually.'

'Why did you wait?' I ask him. 'You've been working here for months now. Why did you wait so long?'

'I wanted to get to know you a little,' he tells me. 'To be honest, I only intended working with you for a week or two. But then there was Louise. I could see how close you were, and she was retiring soon anyway. I thought I'd see the internship through until she was gone.' He sighs, as if years of pain have come to an end, slaps his hands down on his knees, offers a half-smile, and stands up. 'Anyway. There we are.'

'Sit down,' I snap. For the first time since he arrived at the hospital, I don't want him to go away.

'No,' he says calmly. 'I've said all I needed to say. It's time now.'

'Time for what?'

'To report you. First to the authorities here in the hospital. Then to the police. I've already made an appointment. I imagine they'll be in touch.' He glances at his watch and, to my surprise, simply leaves my office without another word.

I stare at the closed door, trying to figure out what to do next. In a moment, I'm on my feet, running towards it, flinging it open, and am charging down the corridor after him. I pass Michael, who raises an eyebrow in surprise, and see Aaron stepping into the elevator. He turns around and smiles as he sees me rushing towards him.

And that's when I realize that he's not alone in there.

There's another man standing next to him. Someone who, I assume, has been waiting in the corridor throughout our conversation, knowing that today is my day of reckoning.

They're both looking at me.

I'm ready to give up my fear of enclosed spaces. There are bigger things to be frightened of. I charge towards them, ready to rip the doors apart with my bare hands if I have to, if only I can get to talk to them both, to explain, to stop them doing what they're going to do.

But it's too late.

Aaron turns away. He has no interest in ever looking at my face again.

And his best friend, Hugh Winley, places a comforting arm around his shoulder.

As the doors close, he whispers something to him and Aaron nods and smiles again, before exhaling heavily.

I leave the hospital a few minutes later, knowing that I'll never set foot here again. I don't know when the police will show up. Maybe this evening. Maybe tomorrow. But it will be soon, and when the process begins, I know how it will end. Everything will come out. They won't care about what Arthur and Pascoe did to me, they'll say that I'm a grown woman who made my own choices. I'll be struck off. I'll go to jail. Perhaps they'll even trace Rufus or George back to me. If they do, I'll spend the rest of my life behind bars. Maybe I'll suffer the same fate as Evan Keogh, the boy on whose jury I sat. Found mysteriously dead after a supposed suicide but probably the victim of something more sinister.

I consider my choices. I could go straight to the airport and buy a plane ticket, but I don't know which countries have extradition treaties with the UK and which don't. It would probably take less than two minutes on the internet to find out, but what's the point? It would just keep all of this going and, honestly, I'm so tired.

I could kill myself. I've thought about that before but know that I don't have the courage to do what needs to be done.

I could get disgustingly drunk and, for a few hours at least, I might feel happy, before the nightmare begins.

I glance at my watch. It's just gone three thirty. I get in

my car and drive ten minutes south, in the direction of a local school that gets out around now. I slow down when I see the boys making their way home and wait until I find a suitable one, walking alone, young, vulnerable, and innocent.

I slow down.

I pull over.

He's moving closer and closer, almost in sight now.

I close my eyes and take a deep breath.

I think of Arthur and Pascoe, who raped me and buried me alive.

I think of Aaron, Rufus, George, and all the other boys I've taken home with me over the years.

My finger hovers over the button that will lower the window on the passenger side. I wait until the boy is almost parallel with my car.

Only then do I make my decision.

Fire

is one of
The Elements

Read Willow's story in

Water

Read Evan's story in

Earth

And Aaron's story in

Air

Published by Doubleday
in May 2025

John Boyne is the author of seventeen novels for adults, six for younger readers, and a collection of short stories. His 2006 novel *The Boy in the Striped Pyjamas* has sold more than eleven million copies worldwide and has been adapted for cinema, theatre, ballet and opera. He has won four Irish Book Awards, including Author of the Year in 2022, along with a host of other international literary prizes. His novels are published in sixty languages, making him the most translated Irish writer of all time.

X (formerly Twitter): @JohnBoyneBooks
Instagram: @JohnBoyneAuthor